2 4t

VC
BW

JAN 1 1 2008

A SURFEIT OF SOLDIERS

Paris, 1944. War correspondent Harry Britwell chances across Jan van Vliet, a Dutch Resistance member and old acquaintance, who pleads for his help. Jan's sister Christina has been captured by the *Abwehr* — the German intelligence organisation — in Holland. By threatening to hand her over to the Gestapo, they have forced him into playing the role of double-agent. But Jan's supply of false information to feed them is running out . . . Can he and Harry succeed in entering occupied Holland and removing Christina from the clutches of the enemy?

Books by David Bingley
in the Linford Mystery Library:

LONG RANGE DESERTER
RENDEZVOUS IN RIO
ELUSIVE WITNESS
CARIBBEAN CRISIS
THE PLACE OF THE CHINS

DAVID BINGLEY

A SURFEIT
OF SOLDIERS

Complete and Unabridged

LINFORD
Leicester

First published in Great Britain

First Linford Edition
published 2008

British Library CIP Data

Bingley, David, *1920 –*
    A surfeit of soldiers.—Large print ed.—
Linford mystery library
    1. War correspondents—Great Britain—Fiction
    2. Spies—Netherlands—Fiction 3. World War,
    1939 – 1945—Netherlands—Fiction
    4. Detective and mystery stories
    5. Large type books
    I. Title
    823.9′14 [F]

    ISBN 978–1–84782–066–2

Published by
F. A. Thorpe (Publishing)
Anstey, Leicestershire

Set by Words & Graphics Ltd.
Anstey, Leicestershire
Printed and bound in Great Britain by
T. J. International Ltd., Padstow, Cornwall

This book is printed on acid-free paper

To the indestructible Dutch.

1

Britwell's uncharacteristic hotel siesta in the French capital on Liberation Day, August, 1944, lasted longer than he had intended. When eventually he shrugged off the veils of sleep his mind was temporarily purged of earlier exciting exploits in divers theatres of war. His thoughts were on his pre-war acquaintance-ship with Marie Smith, a half-French half-English dancer, whose company he hoped to enjoy again quite soon.

He had first become acquainted with Marie when his main journalistic involve-ment was still in sport. In fact, he had quite recently varied his output so that some of it could be classed as crime-reporting when, on that sunny spring day in 1939, he had blundered into her in Hyde Park, London. In those days, he still had an interest in pretty girls who were going places, and it had only been the night before when he first saw her dancing on stage with a troupe of young, talented hoofers in a Shaftesbury Avenue theatre.

He yawned and smiled without opening his eyes, as he recollected how he had first seen her in her pale blue track-suit, jogging along with her shoulder-length black hair tied back in a blue ribbon, her heart-shaped face ruddy with the sun and wind, and her green come-hither eyes screened behind a pair of rectangular-lensed sun spectacles.

She had bounced like a gazelle at every step, and he had difficulty in catching up with her, although he was reasonably fit at the time. His sudden determination to make her acquaintance had helped him to match her telling performance and to keep within talking distance while he claimed breathlessly to have met her before.

Marie had accelerated and would have stayed ahead had not an absent-minded old man walking a dachsund on a long lead brought about her downfall by tripping her when she had been glancing back over her shoulder. Britwell then caught up, switched to his most charming manner and began to make headway as he laboured to breath normally. The old fellow had been shooed away. The journalist forcibly accepted the blame for what had happened. He gently massaged her knee; insisted that she took a ride in his car, instead of calling a taxi which she did habitually in these circumstances. And in this way, a pleasant friendship began.

He found himself attending the same theatre fairly regularly, going to parties and sports meetings with Marie and her friends, and having to fend off criticisms at work which suggested that he was still far more interested in sport than in crime.

Within a month of their meeting, through Marie, Britwell was to renew acquaintance with a young Dutch girl, Christina van Vliet, whom he had met at the Berlin Olympics, the *Daily Globe* having sent him there to report on his first really big international sporting contest.

Christina had flopped when swimming the 400 metres free-style for her country.

She had finished sixth, experiencing a falling off in leg power in the last hundred metres. Her coaches had been disappointed in her performance, but as the event was won by a more experienced Dutch swimmer, their disappointment had been short-lived.

Her brother, Jan, who was also an Olympic contender, had made light of her failure, but Christina who seemed to take everything in life so seriously had withdrawn into herself for a while, and only returned to the company of former friends when it was clearly understood by them that she would improve her leg power beyond all recognition and again offer herself as a contender for the same event in the next Olympic Games. But alas, the onset of war had caused the Games to be cancelled indefinitely. The year 1940, had seen Germany, Russia, Great Britain, Italy and other European countries at one another's throats. And the young of these countries were contending for wartime honours in the place of peacetime medals.

Christina in a swim suit, with her

wonderful titian hair hidden in a tight bathing hat, had seemed on early acquaintance to be one of a type of buxom teenage Dutch girl swimmers, tall and freckled, and graceful in movement in spite of her long limbs and the full roundedness about the bust and shoulders common to swimming athletes. However, it was in London, and once again in that same park, that Britwell had been struck by the marked contrast of Christina, the runner.

Marie knew that Britwell was already acquainted with Christina and her brother, Jan. She played a trick on the journalist, withholding the identities of her friends from abroad until the four of them met for that constitutional run in the open air.

Britwell had seen the three of them jogging towards him when they were perhaps a hundred yards apart. Later, he had taken a photograph of them, the same trio smiling and running towards him in their track suits.

Marie herself always graced the park, but Christina, who was about four inches taller and considerably longer in the leg, provided a picture of another sort with that long titian hair spilling out in the morning breeze. Her blue eyes radiated exuberant health and recognition as they came together.

Brother Jan had broken up a warm embrace involving his half-sister and Britwell. Secretly, Britwell had hated him for it, but not for long. Jan van Vliet was a big overgrown, over-muscled, fully extroverted young Dutchman with a total lack of discretion and an aggressive recklessness which had to be experienced to be believed.

For instance, in that same Berlin Olympics, Jan had failed to present himself for the tossing of the hammer and the shot-putting, and practically the whole of literate Europe knew why. He had made the newspapers in a way that Olympic coaches tried to avoid, by getting involved in a road accident after a prohibited drinking bout scarcely twenty-four hours before he was wanted.

Although he was in disgrace, Big Jan's infectious grin, his gusty laughter, his homely features and his crisp curly red hair which stuck up above most people in any crowd, had made him as much a personality in the German capital as the most popular winners of the medals.

Britwell blinked himself awake, glanced at his wrist watch and saw that three hours had passed. So vivid had his recollections been that he felt that he had been dreaming about the trio from the past. He had to reassure himself that Marie was 'for real' by examining once again her likeness on the theatre programme he had acquired earlier.

After that, he dressed himself most carefully, partook of a light meal in the hotel dining room and then resolutely wandered into the street, leaving the comparative comfort of the Rivoli Hotel behind him. He was watchful as he moved away, and mildly furtive in his movements. His aim was to dodge any members of the Civil Affairs team with whom he had entered Paris.

★   ★   ★

On Liberation Night, it was difficult for a stranger to visit a theatre without

7

booking. Even if that stranger was a man in uniform, one who had ridden in with the first of the liberators. The street blackout was maintained, either because of the lack of power or because an illuminated city might draw to itself a barrage of shells from a retiring enemy.

Taxis were few and far between. Britwell covered several hundred metres before he met with success. There were two places on the obvious route to the Champs Elysees which had suffered during the day through shell blasts. In order to avoid the craters, the taxi driver made detours. In one he was caught in a head-on jam with others coming in the opposite direction.

Britwell had to get out and walk on before the dispute was settled as to who should give way. His driver came after him, and faultlessly covered the rest of the journey. The house was full when he arrived. Even if some failed to take their seats or others left early, there would be others ahead of the lone Englishman for the privilege of using their places. An articulate receptionist explained as much.

A few steps ahead of an *agent de police* Britwell made it to the manager's office. There, he claimed acquaintance with the youthful manager's father, since retired. That excuse did away with a possible sudden eviction.

The music from the stage spilled out occasionally towards the office, so that Britwell and the *directeur* could tell without effort which of the groups of entertainers were in action. As for getting near to the action, further progress was slow. An appeal to the *directeur's* sense of occasion failed. He was unimpressed with a press card backed up by a personal letter from a brigadier at the War Office. It was only when Britwell lost patience and began to hint at his intention to take Mademoiselle Marie away from her regular work for a prolonged holiday that Jacques Thibault (Junior) began to realise that he could not withstand the demands of this renowned British war correspondent with the quiet manner.

During the last session, when *les Papillons* and Marie in particular, were holding forth on the stage, Britwell was directed to a ladder to one side of the wings. He clambered up it, and emerged onto a makeshift stage balcony to the left of the stage proper. Two tables were occupied by half a dozen servicemen like himself, except that they were mostly French or Americans.

Down below *les Papillons* were sending the audience into ecstasies with a succession of saucy dances concluded by the can-can. The whole theatre was ringing with the excited yells and hoots of the Parisians as Marie and her girls sank down for the last time into the splits.

Round upon round of applause. Curtain after curtain. The manager appeared eventually, saying that the girls were tired: that Marie's voice was affected. One of the stand-up comedians led the audience in community singing so that les girls were free to retire.

Some ten minutes later, Jacques Thibault, backed by a stage-door keeper who happened to be an ex-wrestler, kept upwards of a dozen would-be suitors away from Marie's door. Thibault smuggled Britwell along to the room as soon as they had gone.

He said: 'Monsieur Britwell, it was no joke when I said to the audience Marie was tired. If you truly have her welfare at heart, you will be gentle with her.'

Britwell nodded. Thibault knocked on the door, opened it and pushed him inside. He closed the door, whipped off his forage cap and grinned shyly at Marie who was draped languorously over a chaise-longue with a glass of white wine in her hand. Her green eyes rounded in surprise, almost as though she felt trapped. And then, very slowly she relaxed, and attempted to rise.

'Harry Britwell, of *all* people! Where have you been all this war? What kept you?'

He gestured for her to stay where she was, hurriedly crossed over to the chaise-longue and knelt beside her, taking her hand in his and kissing it. She drained her glass, dropped it to the floor and threw her arms about his neck in a warm embrace. They kissed twice before she gently disentangled herself. He sat on the couch beside her, still holding her hand.

'It's been a long war, Marie. I've seen a

lot of places, lost a lot of friends. But I'm glad to see you're still as good as ever, and still stunning the patrons.'

His keen eyes were taking in every detail of her. Her figure was still superb. If anything, she was a pound or two lighter than he remembered her. Her intense green eyes had acquired slight shadows apart from her make-up. He wondered what the wartime occupation had done to her.

She had just started to talk about her experiences when the door was suddenly thrown open. In came two stern-looking men in British army uniform, followed by the *agent de police* who had earlier prowled the foyer.

Britwell shot to his feet and rounded upon them. The first was a stocky major with a greying waxed moustache. The other was a tall, fair lieutenant whose grey probing eyes ranged the chaise-longue, the chairs, the make-up dressing table, the wardrobe and the dusty metal filing cabinet against the rear wall.

Britwell said icily: 'What is the meaning of this intrusion? An entertainer is entitled to some privacy in her dressing room.'

The major nodded to the policeman who retired, closing the door behind him. The lieutenant continued to drum with his fingers on the leather of his pistol holster. Eventually, the major took a couple of steps forward with his hands behind his back.

'I'm Major Petham, Army Intelligence. We're here on official business. Kindly explain who you are.'

Marie, who had been clad only in brief matching pants and bra with a silver sheen, reached for her cloak of the same material and draped it round her shoulders. She placed her feet on the floor and faced them, tight-lipped and apprehensive, her arms crossed over her breasts.

Moving with infinite slowness, Britwell produced from his tunic pocket his press card and the letter from the War Office. He handed them over and noted with satisfaction that the major was impressed by the brigadier's signature. The lieutenant read the details over his superior's shoulder.

Britwell resumed: 'I'd be obliged if you'd tell me the nature of your business, major. Mademoiselle Marie is a close personal friend of mine going back to peacetime.'

Petham briefly considered the request. All the time he was thinking a small muscle was twitching at the side of his jaw. Britwell, meanwhile, refilled Marie's glass from the bottle and patted her on the shoulder.

'Oh, very well, Britwell. I think we'd better talk in the manager's office.'

The lieutenant stepped briskly to the door. Britwell murmured to Marie that he would be back. He then followed the two officers out of the room and back to the private office. As they entered Thibault came out from behind his desk and hovered. Invited to stay, he slipped into a chair located in a corner and dabbed at his jowl with a white handkerchief.

With the major in the manager's chair and the lieutenant lounging stiffly nearby, the exchanges began.

'Britwell, you are the first British war correspondent we have encountered in the city. Could you tell me briefly how you came to be here so promptly?'

Britwell nodded, smothered a yawn and sat down in front of the desk. His explanation was brief. He concluded: 'I do have a modest reputation for being well up with the action, sir. Now, perhaps you'll tell me what you expected to find here?'

'You know I don't have to,' Petham began brusquely.

Britwell remained poker-faced, waiting.

'Well, the fact is, we were tipped off. Our informer told us that a very doubtful character, a double agent, had made contact with Mademoiselle Marie this very evening. We wanted to lay hands on him. He was said to be in British uniform and, frankly, we thought we had him.'

After a wide general experience with most branches of the forces in wartime, Britwell was a difficult man to surprise. On this occasion, however, he *was* surprised. This talk of double agents, and the apparent implication of Marie Smith had him baffled. He found himself thinking rather melodramatically of treason, traitors and spies.

He replied cautiously. 'You think perhaps that some, er, informer, knew that I had visited Marie and mistook me for someone else?'

Petham sniffed. 'I think now it's very probable. Even though you had not been with her long. Thibault assures me she had no other visitors before you arrived.'

'You surely don't think Marie is a traitor of sorts to the country of her birth, major? And surely agents in Paris will be out of the action, now. Are you suggesting that there's still a need for spies when the Germans are being steadily pushed back to their own borders?'

'Marie Boyer — she married a French airman, by the way, and is widowed now. Madame Boyer is not thought of as a traitor, but she does have contacts. Friends in the countries still occupied by the enemy. If you've known her since peacetime, that shouldn't surprise you. The underground war, of course, contin-ues. In liberated France we need to know about collaborators and such. From countries ahead of our armies, we need first class information. But all that should

16

not concern you.'

Petham's tone became suddenly brusque. He glanced obliquely at his subordinate, the lieutenant, who cleared his throat in a somewhat perfunctory fashion and glared at Britwell.

'We must remind you never to write about matters of Intelligence, Britwell. Furthermore, any failure to report to us information subsequently gleaned about Marie Boyer's doubtful contacts could result in your being relegated to a desk job in U.K.'

Britwell nodded slowly. He swallowed his wrath, and studied the junior officer's pale face. He supposed that had he been born a German the fellow would have made a good Abwehr man, a member of the counter-intelligence corps.

He said: 'Thank you for reminding me of my duty, lieutenant. I'm impressed. In fact, I shall probably remark upon your thoroughness the next time I visit the war office. If that's all, gentlemen, I'll take my leave now.'

He stood up, thinking briefly of his own skin, in contrast, so recently darkened by the intensive Burma sun: his sun-bleached fair hair and the white crowsfeet wrinkles at the outer corners of his eyes. The veiled threat underlying his words did not pass undetected by his interrogators. Thibault's eyebrows were still raised as the war correspondent left the room.

★   ★   ★

In Marie's dressing room, he studied his profile in the mirror while the dancer finished dressing in a dark trouser suit which hid her feminine contours and gave her a youthful manly look. He could see that she was anxious to get away from the building to her lodgings.

The patrons had left. The dressing room area was exceedingly quiet when the solid muted thump came from the direction of the tall wardrobe. Marie stiffened up in sudden fear. Her eyes went first to the door, and then to Britwell, who crossed rapidly to the article of furniture and opened the door.

He stepped back in surprise, bereft of speech. Coiled up inside it, with his legs higher than his head was a tall bulky figure in khaki clutching a near-empty beer bottle in his right hand. The close-cropped red head was bare. The homely features built around the backward curving nose betrayed the pallor of fatigue and yet, even in the shadow, they were familiar to Britwell, who identified the stranger at once.

His mind was full of new conjecture as the fellow spilled out sideways, adroitly rolled and rose to his feet and towered above Britwell. Clearly, the chap was to some extent under the influence of liquor, but he was prepared to fight if resistance was necessary.

Marie muttered something in French about the utter foolhardiness of drinking when men were searching for him. The big fellow's recognition was slower than that of his discoverer. He did not start to relax until Britwell had grinned in his face, and extended his right hand.

'Jan,' he murmured softly. 'Jan van Vliet. I can imagine you in all sorts of circumstances, but I never thought to find you playing jack-in-the-box in Marie's dressing room. It's good to see you again, Jan. I'm Harry Britwell. We met in London, in case your memory is at fault.'

Van Vliet tossed the empty bottle onto the chaise-longue. He shook Britwell's hand with a force which threatened to crush the bones. Marie had to push herself between them to bring Jan back to a sense of their present predicament.

'Jan, we have to smuggle you out of here, at once. Damn it, you're one of the luckiest fools I know. Anyone other than Harry Britwell finding you here would have meant serious trouble for you, for *me*, too.' She turned to Harry. 'You'll help me to get him away, Harry? For old time's sake, if nothing else?'

Britwell found himself nodding, acting under the remarkable spell of Marie Smith Boyer. He wondered what he was letting himself in for.

2

Jan van Vliet fought off the alcoholic haze and at once put himself at the disposal of Marie. While Britwell stood with his back to the door, the bulky Dutchman pulled the metal filing cabinet away from the wall. Behind it was a low narrow door, camouflaged by wallpaper of the same colour as the rest of the room.

Alternately biting her lip and delicately shifting her dancer's legs, Marie whispered her instructions.

'Get out through the back way, Jan. Here are the keys of my car. Get in the rear and cover yourself with the blanket which you will find there. We shall have to leave the building by the side entrance. And remember, if anything goes wrong we don't know anything about you. We can't be implicated. Is that understood?'

The instructions had been given in English. Britwell reflected that Marie, fluent in most European languages, could have spoken in another tongue. By what seemed a miracle, the great body of the Dutchman folded and appeared to contract as he moved into the short dark passage beyond the secret door.

Marie was breathless with relief after he had gone. She clung briefly to Britwell and he could feel her trembling through her clothes.

'Please, Harry. Don't ask any questions. Push the filing cabinet back into place and come away with me. I — I just hope I don't land you in any trouble. Are you — will you help?'

Britwell closed the secret door and heaved the cabinet back into place. This clandestine operation was a far cry from anything he had anticipated when he rode into Paris with the Civil Affairs team. He wondered where it would all end.

The muscular stage-door keeper was seated on the steps outside the stage door. He was methodically feeding himself with a French stick of bread and a useful wedge of cheese, while his battered ears took in the distant sounds of merriment across the relieved city.

He shifted over as the couple came out of doors. He noted the way in which his favourite dancer clung to the arm of the Englishman. He was used to her street disguise, amounting to a trouser suit and a dark beret, but usually she came away alone. Often, he went round the back and brought her car round from the car park. He wondered what this Englishman had that so many other would-be suitors apparently lacked.

Without pausing to exchange pleasantries, the girl hurried off with her escort. '*Bonsoir*, Francois. You'll be celebrating when you get home, I suppose. *A bientot.*'

No pause, in consideration of his reply. They vanished almost at once, and shortly afterwards, the black popular-model Renault left the park and went off towards the west.

* * *

Marie's flat was two kilometres away, in the basement of a huge drab stone apartment block. The *concierge*, a woman, had her office and flat at street level, which meant that the dancer was able to enter and leave the building without being checked or observed. Marie's hours, always irregular, failed to occasion any special comment in the building on account of her job.

Jan slept on the brief journey. He was snoring when they pulled up in front of the building and the business of smuggling him into the flat could have been very tricky indeed. As Britwell staggered from the curb supporting most of Jan's weight, he found himself wondering how Marie would have coped, had he not been with her. Luck was with them. Windows overhead were wide open and flags fluttered at every level, but most of the tenants had gone off to the boulevards to dance and sing their way through the night.

Marie had a bathroom, one bedroom, a living-room with a kitchen alcove and a small spare room which she used to store things in. Jan flopped lifelessly on the bed and resumed his deep sleep which had been disturbed for the staggering entry.

Britwell returned to the car, collected a

few private items belonging to the girl and locked it up. He gave her a *Gitane* cigarette, and lighted a small cigar for himself, while they waited for the kettle to boil. After sipping two cups of coffee apiece, Marie moved into the bathroom where she washed and changed into a gold pair of pyjamas and a pleated housecoat of the same colour.

Devoid of make-up, she looked palely beautiful and at the same time vulnerable. Her troubled green eyes closely explored Britwell's face as they kissed, their silent union punctuated by the Dutchman's snores. The girl expected some initiative from him, and he did not fail her.

Sprawled in her armchair, and minus his tunic, he waved his small cigar in the direction of the bedroom. 'Marie, I don't know what you're up to or how deeply involved you are with Jan. I don't regret anything I've done tonight, but I feel I'm owed a few explanations. Especially if you are still counting on my assistance, and discretion. For old time's sake, as you said earlier. I need some answers. And you can't afford to have Jan around very long, especially if he's done what I think he has. So what do you say? I'd like to be able to ease the burden you seem to be carrying before I have to move on.'

Marie fumbled in her housecoat pocket, produced a small neat cigarette holder into which she inserted her *Gitane*. She sniffed and nodded. 'I thought you'd say something like that, Harry, knowing your character and all. I think we ought to bring Jan awake. He has a most unusual story to tell, and it might sound better coming from his own lips.'

Britwell nodded. Between them, they inserted a towel under the sleeping man's head. A wet hand towel and dribbling water failed to rouse him and eventually they had to drag him off to the bathroom and run the shower attachment over his head and shoulders.

After a solid fifteen minutes work, he began to respond. His glazed eyes took in the pair of them, their sober expressions, and when he started to blink his eyes and furrow his brow over the coffee they knew that he was thinking deeply about his predicament.

Britwell was the one to check that they were not overheard at the door and windows. He started the discussion.

'Jan, the events of this evening have surprised me. By what I've already learned, you must have been working as some sort of an agent with the Dutch Resistance. Furthermore, Marie, here, seems to be involved. In your shoes, I'd think very seriously before putting my girl friends into such an invidious position.

'Those Intelligence officers who pushed their way into Marie's dressing room spoke of a double agent wearing British uniform. Now, that's a different matter altogether. A member of the Dutch Resistance could be doing a great job of work, but a *double* agent! Hell, Jan, I know how you were in peacetime, reckless and irresponsible to say the least, but the type to turn a traitor? Never. I need explanations, and I'm waiting.'

Jan discarded his empty cup. He glanced briefly from one friend to the other and then back again. His big spatulate left hand massaged his scalp through the short red hair.

'And why are you here, if your business is in Holland and Germany?' Britwell added, in the short silence.

A bit of the old arrogance lit up Jan's face at this last query.

'I am here because I wanted to come out for a rest. You may think me a fool, Harry, but I can assure you that I am a past master at crossing frontiers, if and when I please. I came also, because I was worried. On the face of things, I *am* a double agent. But I haven't given to the Germans any information they didn't have already. I want you to believe that because it is true. Maybe I was a fool to seek out Marie, but she knew me well and she knew Christina also. I thought she would understand about what I had been forced to do.'

'What exactly have you done, Jan, to put the British against you?' Britwell persisted, in a low voice.

Jan waved his big hands to gain a little time. Marie, too, seemed to give the impression that Britwell was rushing things.

'For two or three years the Dutch

Resistance has done a great job for the Allies. Only, well, the war has gone on a long time. It becomes inevitable that here and there German infiltrators get an inkling of what is going on. They penetrate the cells of the Resistance fighters.

'This has been happening in the early part of this year in various areas of Holland. British airmen being secretly moved from one cell to another have been picked up by the enemy, along with the members of the cell. Those of us who were still active and apparently not known to the Abwehr had to be more and more careful.

'In order to facilitate one escape, I called on my sister, Christina. Up until that time, she had confined her activities to hospital work and occasionally running errands. I brought her into it because we were trying to get the flyers out by another route, by a small port on the coast, south of the Hague.'

Britwell began to perspire as his thoughts ran ahead of the explanation. 'Are you trying to tell me that Christina was taken by the Gestapo while she was working for you?'

Van Vliet sighed and nodded very decidedly. 'That is exactly what I am trying to tell you. The Abwehr took her. I had to act quickly to try and save her, so I went to an officer I knew to be in charge of counter-intelligence for central Holland. A Major Ernst Grunfeld of Abwehr IIIF, in Dreibergen.

'I told him what I had been doing, and fed him certain information about Dutch Resistance cells as had already been infiltrated and dispersed. On the understanding that Christina, a relatively innocent party, was released before the Gestapo got their hands on her.'

Britwell and Marie moved closer together on the settee. He found himself gripping her limp hand with undue pressure.

Marie murmured: 'He isn't sure, but he thinks Grunfeld will keep his word. Christina is probably free at this moment. She'll be watched, of course, after this. And Jan will have to work to order for his new masters. Otherwise, any known relatives might suffer. You see how it is, Harry? He did it for Christina. I think you'd have done the same in similar circumstances. Wouldn't you?'

He nodded and favoured her with a brief smile. 'To be honest with you, I had thought my interest in this war was totally dead. Now, I'm not so sure. I'd like to do something for Christina, but I don't see how it's possible. How long will it take for the allied armies to overrun Holland?'

Jan's wide mouth smiled without warmth. 'So that Christina will be safe? Who knows? In ordinary circumstances, a few weeks. A month or two. I have to go back into Holland again. One piece of information my German master asks for, and I do not have it.'

'What is that?' Britwell asked curiously.

'Exactly when and where the Allies will make an airborne assault beyond the present fighting line. If you knew, would you tell me, Harry, so that I could keep Christina out of the Gestapo's clutches?'

Britwell groaned. 'Poor Jan, you really have got yourself in a fix. No, I couldn't tell you, even if I knew such a thing. Nor could you, I think, if you knew the exact time and place. If you can come and go as easily as you say, go back to Holland, make up a fictitious time and place, and spirit Christina away before there's time for you to be proved wrong.'

'Good advice, old friend, but not an easy assignment, you'll allow,' Jan replied grimly, all the time wagging a broad index finger at the other two. 'I don't think I'm giving away any secrets when I say all three of us in this room love Christina to some degree. How would you like to put yourself in my hands, Harry? Come with me this very day, back to my country, Holland, to help spirit Christina away to safety!' He turned his ardent eyes to Marie. 'Help me to persuade him, Marie. Please.'

Jan was a big uncouth man. Britwell supposed that he had never pleaded with anyone for anything since he was a small boy. Jan was an outsize character; some would say he was larger than life. At that moment in time it was clear to his listeners how very dearly he loved his long-limbed half-sister, Christina.

Britwell shifted, feeling at once tired and uneasy. He had become the focus of attention. The other two knew he was thinking hard, and they gave him time to come up with his answer.

'If you think I'm a coward for saying no to your scheme, Jan, you are probably right. But I could produce other reasons. My brother, Jack, died just a short while ago in Normandy. I've loved and lost people — both men and women — in vastly different circumstances. I'm saying that as time goes by I've become something of a Jonah, on occasion. I fear I might be the one to put you in the hands of your enemies.

'No, I won't come with you. But I will try to get into Holland in my own way. Ahead of the ground forces, if at all possible. You've trusted me with a lot of information. Before we part, perhaps you could suggest where to look for Christina?'

Jan chuckled. He whispered: 'I thought you were keen on my sister. Of course I'll give you some details. But first we must sleep. Me, with a blanket on the floor. You two make your own arrangements.'

One moment, he was upright. The next, so it seemed, he had blacked out the flat and extinguished himself. To the surprise of Marie and Britwell, the two of them quickly drifted off into sound sleep, although the confines of the single bed and their mutual embrace should, in ordinary times, have precluded such a phenomenon. It was not until Marie whimpered in her sleep that they came sufficiently awake to become once more totally aware of each other.

The love-making which followed was at once passionate and gentle, and when it was over Britwell denied himself the privilege of asking her which of her fears had caused the nightmare.

3

Britwell left Paris at an early hour the following day, spurred on by a new sense of urgency. Marie and Jan had surprisingly renewed his flagging interest in war. Furthermore, his past — which had seemed so remote — and the people who had figured in it, had become real to him again.

All the way back to Calais in a bouncing truck, troubled thoughts concerning the possible fate of Jan's half-sister, the tall auburn-haired and delectable Christina van Vliet, warred with his efforts to compose pieces on the liberation of Paris for his newspaper.

The sea was choppy. A veteran ferry bucked and wrestled its way across the famous narrows to Dover and England. The weather came between the man and his intended outpourings. He gave himself over to sleep, temporarily abandoning his half-composed despatches.

The jubilant wounded who travelled with him thought him strangely withdrawn. For them it was a trip in the right direction, to a U.K. hospital and possibly to an honourable discharge which would return them permanently to their families.

Britwell, by contrast, was mentally girding himself up for another big effort. What he had learned from the lips of Jan van Vliet about the possibility of a huge allied airborne invasion of Holland quite intrigued him. At the same time, the secret knowledge isolated him from his fellows.

All through the next day when he was preparing and redrafting copy and attempting to justify his fleeting visit to the French capital his thoughts were on Christina: how she had been in the Berlin Olympics: her maturing personality in 1939, and how she must be now, with German counter-espionage agents watching her every move. He sensed her vulnerability. His deep feeling for her, and his promise to Jan gave him the patience and stiffened him again to fight for the privilege of going abroad with the advance airborne strike troops on a top secret mission.

★ ★ ★

In spite of his great efforts at diplomacy, the days started to slip away. As his frustrations mounted, he experienced deep depression. For two whole days he knocked on doors. Two offices admitted him, but the resulting interviews with junior officers came to nothing. Eventually, a certain War Office brigadier, 'Jack' Hobbs, who had been his brother's C.O. in Italy, cordially interviewed him. The meeting was a warm one, but nothing came of it other than a hint to try certain central and southern airfields where parachute training might be taking place.

This, Britwell was quick to do. He contrived a place on a parachute training course two days after the Allies liberated the Belgian capital, Brussels. From Brussels to the Dutch border was no great distance for the ground assault troops to recapture, and he thought he might be too late to help Christina, even if his present luck changed completely . . .

★ ★ ★

Although Britwell was agile, the parachute course taxed him physically. No
one was particularly helpful. Instructors
put pressure on him because he was the
only 'civvy' in a school for sky troops.
Fellow trainees as well as instructors
critically watched his efforts. The squad
jumped from a trapeze into a sand pit.
That was followed by aperture drill, using
dummy plane fuselages. Another day they
were transported to a nearby establishment with a seventy-foot jumping tower.
There, they experienced the first genuine
sensation of free-falling.

Three more frustrating days later it was
balloon jump time. An old comrade, Mick
Judd, promoted sergeant since Burma,
tipped him off before reveille that an
airborne commando officer was coming
to inspect the balloon descents. And that
tip-off prompted Britwell to seek an
interview with the visitor about joining
the all-important Dutch assault force. But
Major Brant, the observer, not only
turned down flat Britwell's request, he
also greatly angered him. The short
meeting ended in uproar.

Britwell's furious voice carried to an American officer who was outside, trying to locate him. The Yankee accent followed him as he stormed away from the building. 'Hey, Britwell, Mick Judd said for me to talk to you! Hold on a minute, will you?' That was the breakthrough.

★ ★ ★

Captain Sal Costanza, U.S.A.A.F., was a pilot based less than fifty miles away, a man with inside knowledge. Moreover, he was the devoted cousin of a girl named Benita who, the previous year, had been all set to marry a U.S. glider pilot named Sandy Malone. Malone, who had died with a broken neck on the occasion when his glider had crashed in the Burmese jungle one dark night early in 1944 containing Mick Judd, Harry Britwell and quite a number of others.

Consequently, Costanza helped. Britwell left the British airborne base immediately and betook himself to a village near the United States Troop Carrier Command Station where Costanza was serving as a senior pilot of bombers. There, even the locals who were relaxing on the right side of harvest knew that something was afoot. Farmers and farm labourers were vying with one another in the pubs about how the weather was likely to be in the near future.

A jeep came out to the pub to collect Britwell on the afternoon of September 16th. By this time, he was mildly confident that the phoney war he had been forced to conduct to get himself abroad with the allied airborne forces had been won. His spirits rose as Sal Constanza met him on the tarmac, introduced him to a lean colonel with a southern accent and explained that he was to go along with a part of the 82nd U.S. Airborne Division as an official observer.

The lean colonel, whose sun glasses were a deeper tint than those Costanza wore, eyed Britwell critically.

'Mr Britwell, I hear tell you once made a landing by glider in Burma?'

'That's perfectly true, sir, and on that occasion the transport was provided by Uncle Sam.'

The colonel chuckled, and fanned himself with a batch of papers clipped to a piece of board. 'Okay, Britwell, the experience will come in handy. You'll be doin' it again before you're much older, only this time it won't be Burma and it won't be dark.'

'I do thoroughly appreciate the chance to go along with your men, sir, and I know you won't expect me to go out of the base or make any 'phone calls after this.'

'You have a sharp mind, young fellow. Business *is* that close.'

Costanza took Britwell along to his mess, saw him settled in, bought him a drink and left him to his own devices. That evening, Costanza had to fly a mission. The bombers left for the continent in a clear sky. The ground staff was buzzing with conjecture. They seemed to have forgotten that it was Saturday night, except that the squad around the bowling alley in the games room were running bets on the following day's weather.

Britwell stayed up late, drinking slowly

and listening all the time. He had been accepted on Costanza's say-so and the personnel talked freely in front of him. Rumours crept into the room from the meteoriligical experts, and the news was good for missions over the Low Countries.

In his bunk, his thoughts turned to his last conversation with Jan van Vliet. The Dutchman's German Abwehr contact, a certain Major Ernst Grunfeld, was last known at a place called Dreibergen. Christina's mother, Nel Broekman van Vliet, lived in Utrecht, while her father, Cornelis van Vliet, was a native of Zutphen, further east, in the province of Gelderland. His work as a railway official kept him away from home quite a lot. There had also been mention of Christina's grandmother who resided at Apeldoorn, further north than the other locations.

It occurred to Britwell as he turned over these locations before dropping off to sleep that he would be on a hiding to nothing in his search and, that once having landed safely in Holland he would need the devil's own luck to make contact with the girl.

★   ★   ★

At 1400 hours, he was seated in the port side of a big roomy glider with a score of American troops, awaiting take-off. The early morning fog had been slow to clear, but nothing had dampened the spirits of the flying soldiers who had been awaiting a chance like this for several weeks. Already many towing aircraft had taken off, and only a slight delay was incurred in the second phase of the big airlift due to the towing planes being slow to line up.

Britwell experienced a few inner qualms as the towing plane revved up and the towing hawser tightened and jerked the glider. The engine noises up ahead faded and then roared afresh. The Horsa romped forward like a panicked bullock. It rose, jerked and wallowed some more and finally settled down to the uncomfortable motion necessary to climb the sky and take its place with the other members of the flying bovine herd.

Britwell's hunched position was the furthest aft on the port side. Next to him was a bulky officer with a captain's silver bars who had his rather disturbing grey eyes fixed on the rest of the squad, and yet stayed aloof from them.

As the Horsa levelled out, Britwell had produced the green-tinted sun spectacles which had served him in two campaigns and polished them. Having put them on, he expected to be alone with his thoughts while the air armada headed roughly east at about 150 to 200 knots. But this was not to happen.

A bony elbow caught the Englishman in the ribs as his neighbour wriggled about and made certain adjustments to his attire. Other troopers, those sitting further up the port side and opposite, watched the captain, much to his amusement.

He unfastened his headgear, clipped a pair of half spectacles on his nose and massaged his pointed ears. 'Don't mind me, amigo. I'm a sort of intelligence officer with this outfit. They're rather wary of me, call me the Professor, 'cause that's my peacetime occupation. Understand? I guess you do. Me, I'm told you're a W.C. Am I right?'

Britwell nodded. In all his long experience this was the first time he had heard a war correspondent referred to as a W.C. He smiled. At least, this former professor was a little different from the common run of American officers. He had a sense of humour. Maybe he had a lot of information to impart.

Chuckling inwardly, the Professor, whose real name was Dwayne Deakin, resumed. 'In a few minutes, I'm goin' to digest the contents of the most secret orders for this operation. I mean mentally digest them of course. But first off, in case you're suffering hell inwardly on account of not knowing quite what we're doing I could talk you through the early stages. I'm sure that would help a man in your situation, only don't go an' croak after I put myself out, will you? On account of all this information wasted, if you know what I mean . . . '

In his lecturer's voice, Deakin began his explanation.

'Aircraft and gliders from fourteen U.S. and eight British airfields are in the process of ferrying an airborne army across to Holland. That much I guess you already know. What you may not know is that they are homing on two main routes. Firstly, they make for rendezvous marked by Eureka Beacons over March and Hatfield. After that, the northern group go out over the North Sea after negotiating another marker at Aldeburgh on the East Anglian coast. The others go via North Foreland, wide of the Thames Estuary.'

Britwell who this far was not particularly impressed by the revelations, nevertheless showed a keen interest and encouraged the captain to go on. He added: 'I must confess I'm more interested in where we're going than any other details.'

'You have the look, young fellow, of a man who is going out on a heavy date! Still, you asked me a question of sorts. We're Jim Gavin's 82nd Airborne Division an' our section is the middle one. We'll be responsible for the crossings over the Maas River at Grave and the Waal at Nijmegen.

'General Max Taylor's 101st Airborne Div will land further south and take care of the water crossings between Eindhoven and Grave.'

Britwell, who was ahead of him in his thoughts, put in: 'That leaves the 1st British Airborne Division and they'll be dropped further north. Their objective can only be the crossing over the *Neder Rijn*, in and around Arnhem. Am I right?'

Captain Deakin's glinting grey eyes revealed a new interest in his listener. 'Why, yes, that's right. The British *are* going to the Lower Rhine at Arnhem. The aim of the exercise is to open up a corridor sixty miles in length so that the ground forces massed on the Dutch-Belgian frontier can move swiftly north and trap German troops located further west in Holland.'

'In addition,' Britwell added, 'if such an operation is a success the German West Wall can be outflanked, and a steady push made for Berlin. This could shorten the war, and the bases of the V-two missiles could be located without delay. It sounds good. I wonder what the chances are of success?'

Deakin's strong forte was a finely-trained memory. Matched by a brain as fluent and resourceful as his own, he began to tire. Although he was not showing it, the stress of the coming landings was affecting his morale. He, therefore, curtailed the discussion soon after it had started and produced from a thin soft leather brief case hidden within his combat clothing a neat stapled sheaf of papers.

Typed across the top of it, quite unmistakably, were the words *Not to be taken in the air*. It was headed, TOP SECRET, dated and titled 'Operation Market.'

Deakin shuffled in his seat, adjusted the trim of his half-glasses and began to read. The daylight in the packed fuselage was shadowy and indistinct. Nevertheless, the American officer started to read, and once he had started he became thoroughly absorbed.

Britwell, after reading a few lines out of

his eye corners, started to assess what he had learned. As near as he could remember all the possible locations connected with Christina's relations were in the northern sector, the one to be tackled by the British.

Some time later, he was wondering about the snags of moving across Holland without benefit of an escort when the plane and glider cleared the Dutch coast and the pattern of jolting, lurching and rattling rather subtly changed.

The pilot increased his revolutions so that they were travelling at another fifteen miles per hour. The yawing motion in the glider grew worse, and to stretch the glider troops' nerves even more taut, the unmistakable crack of exploding shells carried to them. Puffs of grey smoke spoiled the neat blue of the sky.

German artillery located in south Holland had pin-pointed the northernmost of the twin air corridors and was systematically banging away, having had several hours in which to get prepared since the first of the marauding parachutists moved in and made their presence felt.

A touch of the devil got into Britwell's thoughts as the critical time began. In a voice which carried, he remarked: 'What do you think it is, Captain? Could it be fireworks? Some sort of a celebration for liberation day?'

Some G.I.s scowled at him. Others looked away. He wished he had not made the ridiculous remark. The Professor, for once, had no words with which to answer.

4

Following his abortive run to Paris late the previous month and his energy-draining efforts to get back into the war ahead of the ground forces, Britwell now knew with instant certainty that the all-out combat was on again. His thoughts ranged over that previous glider landing in Burma beyond the Shan Hills. There, the enemy had been the alien terrain, amply backed up and strengthened by darkness.

Here, the conditions were radically different. Daylight and, waiting below, the most formidable of the three nations which had been lined up against Britain in this protracted war. The Germans. The fighting men of a mighty nation, men who could fight as well in retreat as when their tails were up in the early days of the war.

Bursting shells peppered the sky with steady and sickening regularity. Avoiding action was scarcely possible for planes of the air armada towing gliders. There were parachutes available to all the personnel in the glider, but with the enemy fully alerted on the afternoon of a fine Sunday Britwell hoped that they would not be called upon to go down individually, sitting ducks under a slow swinging silk canopy, dropping steadily within range of accurate automatic weapons.

The uneven ground to air struggle went on, intensified. Even the most optimistic of the sky troops must have realised that casualties were inevitable. Tiny movements, noddings, adjusting of the tunic at the neck. These were the giveaway signs. Captain Deakin removed his half-spectacles with a hand which was unsteady. The batch of papers was replaced inside his clothing, and his jumping helmet fixed tightly again.

The professor's voice was so low that he had to cup his hand in front of his mouth to talk. 'Britwell, do you think we'll have to make it to earth by parachute?'

'I don't think so, captain. I could be wrong, but I think we're too low to use parachutes.'

Britwell withdrew into himself. He was adjusting his sensitive ears, his whole person to the renewed clamour of bursting shells any one of which might blow this frail glider to pieces if it came too close. The officer in charge of the section, a major, scrambled to his feet on the starboard side, right forward. He banged on the door in the partition which separated the main fuselage from the pilot.

A few seconds later, the glider lurched. The major shot through the door with a hoarse cry. The motion of the engineless plane effectively closed the door behind him. At once, voices were raised full of speculation. It seemed that the officer had been gone an age, that the tow plane and the glider were slowing up in a portion of sky absolutely bracketed by enemy anti-aircraft batteries.

Britwell, who had a large pack on his back and a smaller one on his chest, checked his gear. He was the only man in the group who had no gun with him. The glider bucked and yawed, but not through ordinary air pockets. The shell bursts were apparently getting closer.

Britwell was thinking: Holland is Holland, but it is still in the clutches of the Germans . . .

His thoughts were developing along slightly pessimistic lines when the big crash occurred to port. This time the glider lifted quite suddenly in the air and swung away to starboard. There had been a sort of jarring noise which juddered throughout the whole frame of the craft. Sudden cries of alarm came from men seated about midships on the starboard side. Pointing fingers drew attention to those sitting directly opposite. Two of the men on the port side had died instantly due to splinters from the shell having penetrated the fuselage at their backs. One man's head swung too easily on his neck. Another sat stiffly, his eyes raised, giving an all too lifelike imitation of a man killed from the rear.

An ominous creak, which affected the trim of the glider, gave the first inkling that something serious was wrong. It seemed to come from the exterior. Britwell had just about decided that the port wing was damaged when the officer returned from the pilot's cabin. The pilot, meanwhile, had managed to right the craft after the sudden change of motion accelerated by the near-miss.

The tall major's eyes were shaded by his helmet as he clutched a central overhead rail and called down the length of the fuselage.

'Men, I have to tell you that the flak is getting heavier all the time. The chances are that we may be hit, or that the towing plane will cast us loose before we get to the dropping zone. Whatever happens, panic won't help. And we're too low to parachute, so we have only one course of action.'

He raised one hand and waved it, as though to give his men some extra confidence. Behind him, the pilot opened the door. 'Major, the port wing's fractured! If the towin' pilot don't cast us loose real soon I'm goin' to have to do it myself. A section of the wing is likely to break off!'

The major squatted back in his old spot. The glider side-slipped to port, putting every man's heart in a flutter. The fuselage rocked from side to side, slowly righting itself like a boat filled to the gunwales. The craft juddered as about one metre of port wing tip broke away and spiralled earthwards. At the same time the towing hawser fell away. The pilot began his last death-defying wrestle with the controls.

The flak continued to fly up from all sides. Many flying tugs and their charges had scattered earlier, hoping to get back over the dropping zones by a devious route. In the last two hundred feet of altitude the stricken glider was under the general flak pattern, but two or three light anti-aircraft guns mounted on trucks picked it out as a target and treated it to spasmodic bursts of light shells.

Some hit the port wing again. Others raked the underside of the fuselage and ripped out a jagged patch near the tail. The men crouched low, all their muscles tensed against the sudden impact. Any sort of landing in a glider was rough going, but this one, converted to an irregular screwing motion due to its damage, promised something special in the way of touchdowns.

It came quite suddenly, preceded by a sharp cry of warning from the pilot. The starboard wing, longer by a metre than its counterpart, ripped into the sloping bank of a shallow gully, along which the pilot had attempted to land. The tip crumbled: the craft swung to starboard. Almost at once, the undercarriage touched down and collapsed. The nose and forward fuselage rammed into the heavy tufted soil prevalent in those parts. The nose crumpled inwards like a broken egg shell.

The craft settled. The intense booming sound compacted of rending wood and metal gradually eased down, leaving an unpleasant singing in the ears of the personnel who had been thrown forward and then sideways. Many and loud were the cries and oaths emitted by fighting men from no less than ten different states.

Dust and small debris still flew about. Men sneezed. Others just sat back, breathing hard and feeling a sort of relief.

Deakin produced a small hip flask, swigged from the neck and thrust it under Britwell's nose.

'Bourbon, amigo. The best. Take a swig. It'll do you good!'

As the sounds of the crash faded, so the other, more distant and ominous noises penetrated the wreck and the senses of the survivors. Britwell drank, swallowed hard, and listened. Not very far away, the staccato chatter of a heavy machine-gun reminded them that they had a war to fight. Clearly, they were not the first to strike the reclaimed soil of Holland far away from the scheduled D.Z.

Instead of returning the flask, Britwell rose to his feet and took it along to the major, who then rose to his full beanpole height, brushed it aside and assumed command.

'Men, you know the drill for leaving the glider. Check over your personal kit and weapons and prepare to evacuate! As soon as we are clear, I should like the Professor and Mr Britwell to do what they can for the pilot! Now, let's get going! What's holding you back, we're down, aren't we?'

Britwell glanced towards the pilot's door. Activity all round him made him retire aft, where he drank the major's small portion of bourbon before returning the flask to its rightful owner. As he squatted beside the Professor, a bursting shell raised a crater somewhere wide of the gully. It was considerably closer than Britwell would have liked — assuming that it was aimed at their craft.

Soon, the sky troops were spilling out of the loading door and dropping to the ground. At the outset, being in a gully helped — especially as the enemy was not too far away. The bank provided shelter for them as they emerged and threw themselves to the ground, roughly in arrow head formation.

Britwell raced forward and opened the pilot's door. A sight of appalling chaos met him. In Burma, Sergeant Sandy Malone had already been dead at this stage. This man, a smaller more compact version of Sandy with darker hair, was slumped over his control column gently coughing blood. His olive-skinned face was ashen pale. He looked like a man whose life was fast ebbing.

The Englishman eased him back in his seat. He called for the bourbon and had the satisfaction of hearing the bulky intelligence captain coming towards him. As the cockpit was completely crushed in and the perspex was missing, the staring war correspondent could see as much as, if not more than, the crawling major at the head of the creeping platoon outside.

He called: 'Major, your pilot is very badly injured. What do you want us to do with him? And what are your immediate plans?'

The major was not enjoying having to make emergency plans. He turned to the English voice issuing from the cockpit and answered in a tone which his wife would not have recognised.

'I *know* that, Britwell! So get him out of there! Take him over in that direction, towards the north. There's a cluster of cottages not far off! Maybe you can get help!'

Britwell stuck his head still further through the shattered aperture. He was about to shout for further information when the anxious major resumed. 'I'm taking my men over the meadow towards that strip of woodland dead ahead. That's east, I guess. In the general direction of the D.Z. If we get through all right, I'll send somebody back to make contact with you as soon as possible!'

Abruptly, the major's attention swung away. He harangued his men, urging them up to the rim of the gully. While they were levelling out and getting their breath back, the first of a series of heavy machine-gun bursts came from the direction of the woods.

Britwell sighed and turned his attention to the pilot again. The poor fellow was past conversation. Either the control column or something else of an unyielding nature had pushed in his chest. Captain Deakin began to shout queries and get no answer. As Britwell kicked out the crumpled front shell of the cockpit and saw it slither down the ditch, the discomfited intelligence officer stuck his head into the cockpit and winced at what he saw.

'Captain, I want you to drop out of here and help me lower this pilot down to you. I know it isn't policy to move seriously injured personnel, but we can't just leave him to expire in this wreck. So get a move on, will you? The others are over the hill and into the meadow. The Krauts will come looking for us, and our crash will make it easy for them to locate us!'

'God damn it, you don't say?' Deakin paused long enough to get a few drops of his precious bourbon through the pilot's lips, and then he was scrambling through the riven floor and dropping to the earth. The sky above them was as bright and clear as ever. The incessant tugs and gliders had thinned out for a time. So had the everlasting puffs of smoke engendered by bursting shells.

Now, the exchanges were ground to ground. From the direction of the trees to which the major had been directing his men came more bursts of automatic fire. An occasional muted cry in a foreign tongue suggested that the opposition was organised and likely to become more formidable.

It did. Just as Britwell in a kneeling position was lowering the wounded pilot into Deakin's outstretched arms, the first of a series of light shells burst a few yards away at the top of the bank. Stones and earth flew in all directions.

Britwell drew back, temporarily blinded by the bright flash and the concussing sound. Tiny fragments of twisted metal further perforated the nose of the glider and narrowly missed his kneeling figure. Outside, Deakin did not fare so well. He and the stricken pilot were both hit, first by pieces of metal and then by flying stones, earth and small debris. The side of the bank not far from them blew apart. The Professor did a backward somersault and collapsed with the pilot on top of him.

Blinking himself out of shock, Britwell stared down and witnessed the greater part of the captain's burial. As the minor landslide came to a halt, the Englishman swung himself down, hanging on for more than a minute before dropping himself wide of the new mound with its two bodies.

He landed on his knees only a few inches away from the protruding head of the veteran captain. The formidable grey toughness had faded out of the stricken eyes. He had lost his helmet, revealing a narrow grey widow's peak of hair bisecting his broad forehead. His long-lobed ears looked more pointed than ever. Britwell surmised that he had given his last lecture.

Further down the slope and much nearer the bottom of the new heap, the pilot's right hand also protruded. Britwell's face twisted up with intensified anxiety as he perceived it. The heap might amount to a ton or more in weight. It was between four and five feet high where the two Americans were buried.

Britwell knelt beside the hand and clumsily attempted to check the pulse at the wrist. He thought the pulse had failed, but in his overwrought state he could not be sure. Deakin's voice, reduced to a whisper, spoke close to his ear.

'He's dead. I'm certain of it. I trained as a doctor before I took up college work. As for me, I don't have long. You are in a stronger position. Why don't you just take my dog tags an' push off away from here? Enjoy the fireworks, huh?'

Britwell patted him on the head, straightened up and groaned with frustration. He *had* to do something for the captain. A man couldn't just walk away from another human being almost buried alive in a heap of dirt. His movements punctuated by distant small arms fire and frequent bursts of machine-guns, he searched for and found a tool. It was crude. A long piece of twisted metal which had once been part of the glider.

He pushed it carefully into the earth above the stricken man's head and chest, warned him to keep his eyes and mouth closed, and began to rake away the soil above him. For ten minutes he worked with extreme caution. Deakin cursed him mildly from time to time without having any effect. The hole around the chest was widened and the position eased.

At last, the older man put paid to Britwell's scrabbling efforts.

'Son, it's been nice to have you around, and to know you want to make the effort to save me. But it's not on. My pelvis is crushed. I don't have long. Take the dog tags an' anything else you think you need, and go! Hear me? I'd like to be alone when I give up the ghost.'

'All right, Professor, if that's the way you want it. I'll do that. Those papers . . . and maybe your pistol. And the dog tags. Right?'

Deakin blinked at him once more, forcefully and then gave up the uneven struggle to keep alive. Britwell groaned. He eased up on his labours, dwelt thoughtfully for a minute or more on the unreality of the situation and the marked contrast with his activities in previous weeks, and then he reapplied himself.

It was comparatively easy to open the tunic and release the belt and holster from the waist. The soft leather brief case slid into his hands, too. He was so taken up with the two items that he almost forgot the dog tags. They were round the lean parchment neck of the captain. He stuffed them into the breast pocket of his combat tunic behind which lay the brief case. He knew he was trifling with his future in taking the pistol and holster with him, but from previous bitter experiences he knew that to be completely unarmed had its risks, too.

After placing the captain's helmet over the face and forehead he straightened up and prepared to leave. He scrambled first to the top of the bank over which the major and his men had gone.

Distantly, across a long uneven meadow stippled with stunted shrubs and spiked bushes he could see the fringe of the woodland. No personnel in view, but here and there, briefly, sudden flashes from gun muzzles as the glider troops gave battle with German ground personnel engaging the sky troops who had fallen wide of the dropping zone.

It was still a bright, relatively cloudless Sunday afternoon and the sudden advent of war upon the scene, not the silent battle engendered by occupation any more, but the brutal head-on struggle which preceded liberation, seemed incongruous: completely out of place.

He recollected the major's instructions to go north. There were hedges and ditches for a half mile or more in that direction before the cluster of buildings which probably marked a road.

Britwell dropped down into the gully, crossed it ahead of the wrecked glider and scrambled out on the other side. He had covered perhaps one hundred yards of the uneven polderland soil, liberally sprinkled with low scrub and stunted trees, when he heard the first of the German voices.

It came from ahead of him and to his right. He stiffened and crouched behind a bush, wondering what was best to do. Uppermost in his mind was the fact that he had with him the full secret plans of the allied *Operation Market*. Something had to be done about that.

He had hastily unbuckled the gun belt and was thinking what to do with it when boots rang on stones right ahead of him and two short-tempered German troopers carried out a slanging match. Hurriedly rolling up the belt, he tossed it, holster, pistol and all away to his left where it bounced off a tuft of grass and unwound itself.

To his surprise and consternation, a

trooper rose out of the ground some way behind it and faced directly towards him with a Schmeisser machine-pistol pointing right forward in the steadiest of grips. Other Germans rose into view, so that within a minute he could see that they were in a half circle around him. Some looked pleased at his baffled look of consternation. Others merely wary, or deadly.

His hand went to his tunic, as he wondered whether he ought to make some late heroic move to destroy the papers. Guns clicked. The *feldwebel* nearest to the discarded pistol fired a short burst to one side of his feet. He was still reacting when a second narrow rut was dug on the other side by the same trooper.

'Halte! Lift your hands, *Englander*!'

It was too late to do anything other than obey. He slowly raised his hands, and coolly contemplated the future. He had made it into Holland ahead of the ground troops, but the chances were that he would also be shipped to Germany without ever having seen Christina van Vliet.

5

The trio of old Dutch cottages linked together had long been occupied by a very senior officer of paratroops, his staff, and a handful of Abwehr officers engaged on counter-intelligence work who periodically shifted their base of operations.

The platoon of soldiers who captured Britwell were trained paratroopers working as ordinary ground infantry. He was to learn later that their commanding officer was a certain Colonel-General Kurt Student, a man who had contemplated such an attack as the allies had carried out, but, because his men were thin on the ground, had not been able to do anything specific about an attack from the air.

At first, the prisoner was located in a corridor between rooms with an armed guard at either end. Three officers came out at short intervals from different rooms and looked him over. Already they had the secret plans and the pistol which he had attempted to discard and they were frankly puzzled about him. His war correspondent's flashes counted for something, but his turning up as he did unescorted with comprehensive plans for such an operation as might already be in being made them wonder if he was a spy: if his plans were in some way distorted to fool the German High Command.

A frankly curious *feldwebel* brought out to him a cup of coffee and a German cigarette, both of which he accepted with a good grace. He had a feeling as he drank and smoked that he was being observed, but there were no obvious signs of secret squints and he did his best to keep his nerves in firm control.

Presently, he was taken into a bigger room with white-washed walls, where a major with short dark hair, a broad jaw and piercing eyes was giving all his attention to a mounting heap of recent intelligence reports. The major looked up, gave him a sweeping glance and a curt nod, and then he was back to business, making notes, taking telephone calls, receiving messages and occasionally making calls himself. There was a flap on and no mistake.

A tall, lean, fair lieutenant with a bony forehead and blue eyes ushered him to a seat on the far side of a second desk. As soon as he was seated, the lieutenant took the swivel on the opposite side.

He said: 'Good day to you. I am Leutenant Franz Steiniger, detailed to take down your particulars. You find us rather hard-pressed to keep track of all our duties with our staff diminished, but we shall do our best to treat you properly.'

Britwell thought: So it's to be the soft approach, for a start.

He noted the other's ready smile, which revealed big well-filled gapped teeth, and decided to respond in a like manner.

'Good day to you, leutnant. You're in the Abwehr branch of the armed forces, I suppose?'

This opening question had the leutnant mentally backing off. While Britwell was staring at a blown-up map of the immediate district occupying half a wall, the junior officer shot a swift glance of interrogation in the direction of his superior and received a curt nod.

'Er, yes, I have the honour to serve in the Abwehr. But I was about to ask. Since you have literally dropped into our midst, I wonder if you'd mind explaining yourself a little?'

The lieutenant drew a pad and a pen towards him and waited.

Britwell grinned easily. 'Why, certainly. I don't have any rank or number, you understand, being a journalist. My name is Harry Britwell. I work for the London newspaper, the *Globe*, and I came here with the express purpose of sending despatches back to my paper of the success or failure of the troops I came with.'

Having said that, he leaned across the desk and begged another cigarette which was surrendered with mixed feelings. Steiniger took down what he had said. There was a further unrehearsed delay while everyone in the room listened to the heightened cacophony of action further east. The loud cracks sounded like the exploding of mortar bombs. Some distance further south fighters and fighter bombers were engaged in a short sharp action over the corridor north and south, which the allied 2nd Army was expected to use in the thrust north from the Belgian border.

'Was there anything else, *leutnant?*'

Steiniger smiled again. 'What else did you wish to tell us? Interrogation is our business, of course. If you tell us a lot, we can probably ensure better treatment for you. Our superiors expect us to learn all we can. We try to co-operate.'

Britwell thought: Sure, I bet you do. I wonder if you were educated for a period of time in England, or whether you went to a German university with a good English section.

He said: 'According to the rules of war, I think I have told you all that can be expected. I have found the earlier part of this day tiring and a little disturbing. So if that's all, I'd like to be shown to my room to rest.'

'Please don't be impatient, Mr Britwell.

After all, it could have turned out much worse for you. You could, for example, have died in those woods over there, where most of your American comrades are selling their lives dearly. There's a notion, now. Why should a respectable British war correspondent with nothing on his mind other than his despatches arrive in a U.S. glider, armed with an American pistol and carrying a bunch of papers marked TOP SECRET and *Not to be taken in the air*?

'If you could answer those questions, perhaps we could treat you like an ordinary prisoner of war. Otherwise, well, the possibilities are rather frightening, aren't they?'

Britwell ground out his cigarette. He toyed with his sun spectacles for a few seconds before returning them to his pocket and then he coughed, clearing his throat.

'But you surely don't think I'm a *spy*? I mean to say . . . ' He allowed his voice to tail off, while he appeared to go over in his mind the facts as the Germans knew them. 'Oh, I don't know. Perhaps my arrival may seem a little out of the ordinary. You'll never believe the trouble I had trying to get on this airborne trip. Although I have a few friends in high military places in England, none of them would do anything to enable me to come over with the British. It was only by sheer chance that I managed to thumb a lift with the Yanks.

'The pistol? That was a fool trick, I suppose. I took it from the body of an American officer, a captain, who was dying under a heap of rubble not far from the spot where the glider crashed. *He* brought the secret papers with him, not me. Even now I don't know why I bothered to tunnel under the rubble to get them out of his clothing.

'I mean, well, they're obsolete now, aren't they? Apart from a few details which you couldn't possibly know, unless your contacts are very well informed. If I'd thought they were any real value to the enemy, I could have burned them, or eaten them — in time. After all, I wasn't at all badly shaken by the forced landing. It was just the loneliness that threw my thinking out of gear. After coming all the way from U.K. with a lively bunch of Yanks, everything seemed to go sour.'

He was deliberately under-playing his own intelligence, trying to fool them into bafflement: into serious doubts as to whether the secret plans were genuine, or doctored. Leutnant Steiniger ran out of ideas shortly after that. Right on cue there came a knock at the door.

The door opened and in came an army doctor in a white coat. The major's mien changed. He smiled warmly at the medical man, indicated the presence of the prisoner, and suggested that a screen might be brought in for the medical. This was outside Britwell's expectations. He wondered what sort of a tack the investigation was going off on.

The doctor was a seemingly plump jovial squarehead with no apparent interest in the military side of his work. He toyed with his stethoscope, massaged the bald patch on the flat part of his crown, and chatted away in a high pitched voice which reminded Britwell of a German tenor in a comic opera.

Stripped to his underpants, Britwell submitted to having his chest sounded and his reflexes checked. The screen was on wheels and in a straight line. The end of his temporary cubicle was open, so that his interrogators could easily see what was going on.

The whole affair was exceedingly light-hearted until the doctor noticed the twin grooves on his right hip.

'*Gott im Himmel*, what have we here? Two old wounds. One much older than the other! Such bad luck for a man who's supposed to fight only with words, *mein freund*. I sincerely hope whoever fired those bullets at you was not a German?'

The atmosphere in the room had subtly changed. Britwell could read it in the attitude of the two officers and the N.C.O. who was dawdling over his last signal delivery. No one expected to find war wounds on the body of a bona fide war correspondent. He felt that he was in trouble. He doubted if bluff would help him a lot at this stage.

'I am in good physical condition, *Herr Doktor*, except for these two wounds, which did not escape your attention. In my work, I have a reputation to keep up. I am known as 'Our Man at the Front.' Sometimes, the front is unhealthy for a man looking for exciting despatches.

'I collected the first wound in Italy. The second one was a random shot fired at me on a slope in far off Burma earlier this year. It did not heal as quickly as the first. But that is all. I hope I have collected my last war wound. I think if I had been an American I would have had medals for them. Now, what sort of a grading will you give me to go down on my papers?'

He smiled frankly at the medical man but now, not surprisingly, the doctor's joviality had ebbed. Gripping his stethoscope, the stout man withdrew to the major's desk. There were some short sharp exchanges in guttural German. Most of it was spoken too fast for the prisoner to follow.

He wondered what their next line of approach would be. As he strolled towards his discarded clothes, he received a surprise. The doctor bundled them up and took them away with him. Instead, the N.C.O. tossed over to him an old grey dressing gown, which smelled like discarded German, rather than Dutch.

The poker-faced feldwebel said: 'Now, you will take a wash. In the tub. The kitchen is at the back.'

The other ranks were pressurising him now. At first, he declined to enrobe in the dressing gown, but the N.C.O. hustled him towards the door, obviously impervious as to whether he was clad or not. The doctor had left, and the two Abwehr officers had gone remote. No use protesting to them.

Britwell slipped into the gown and drew it around him. Out in the corridor a thick-set trooper with a beer drinker's complexion and girth hustled him to the rear, jabbing him from time to time with the heavy butt of a rifle.

'*Schnell! Schnell*! Downstairs!'

The prisoner was prodded into the basement of the first house, and then through into the next, the communal wall having been knocked out for convenience. A stiff matronly woman with a lipless mouth looked up from her laundry sorting as he went through. He wondered if she was German or a pro-German Dutch woman.

The room he was eventually taken to was an outhouse: a place where possibly cows had been milked in other times. Two tunicless German privates had filled up an old tin bath with cold water. He was ordered to get in, and when he showed reluctance he was urged along by their booted feet and a few short-arm chops.

One of the attendants went for him with a broom which had stiff bristles, while the other slopped liquid soap over his face and tried very hard to fill his eyes with it. Between them, they had him going for a while. The florid trooper, meanwhile, relaxed and watched. His rolling belly laughs drew the N.C.O. along to watch the sport. Having been hit on the cheekbone by the broom handle, Britwell retaliated, catching the broom head and driving the other end into the olderly's abdomen.

The fellow withdrew, doubled over and gasping. Britwell retained the broom and turned it crosswise to defend himself, using it as a sort of quarter-staff. Suddenly the humour went out of the situation. The other orderly spat out harsh words of protest, addressed to the guards. The trooper reacted by smashing the broomstick out of his hands with a down blow of the rifle.

Britwell rocked on his knees, received fists and knees in his back. Water slopped this way and that, halting the trooper who was watching his opportunity to aim a few jabs with his gun, backed up now by the feldwebel. Roaring with anger, Britwell stepped clear of the bath, upending it so that most of its contents went over the second orderly.

He adopted a defensive stance, feeling more than naked, and awaited a rush which might have ended — so he thought — in his being maimed. Glaring at the N.C.O. he tried a little bluff.

'So, you are all Nazi bullies, *hein? Ist es der Krieg?*'

He was not at all sure as to whether he had properly taunted them about the way they made war, but the sullen orderlies and the armed guards were at least impressed, knowing he understood a little of their language. There was a slight pause, a hesitation, as though they were not quite sure how far they dared to go in roughing up the prisoner. Britwell noted this and seized on it.

'Herr Major!' he yelled. 'Her Major Grunfeld! Your bullies are getting out of hand!'

His shouted words had a magical effect. The N.C.O. straightened his back and became soldier-like again. The winded orderly stopped exaggerating his injury, and the other began to mop up the floor. The trooper grudgingly handed over a fairly clean dry towel. The voice of the major came at them across the small rear paddock.

His queries were answered in short sharp businesslike replies. To Britwell's surprise, the N.C.O. hurried out of the building and came back with the clothes he had been wearing on arrival. Was he in for another smooth period? he wondered. An attempt to get him to say a whole lot more by an apparent show of gentleness?

He dressed himself after drying rather

quickly. In one of the basement rooms he was given coffee and a plateful of stew boosted by two stiff sausages all the way from the Third Reich. There was dark bread and a cigarette to follow and the chance to rest a while. This time he was taken to a room in the third of the three cottages which was absolutely bare, except for a single bed.

Without uttering a single word, the matronly woman he had seen earlier indicated the presence of a guard outside and below the narrow window. The trooper with the boozer's complexion resumed his guarding duties outside the bedroom door.

It was still early evening. Not more than six o'clock, Britwell surmised, his watch having stopped without warning. Further to the east the sky was bright with countless explosions. He knew as he tried unsuccessfully to peer round the angle of the window that the distant crashes and bangs had nothing whatever to do with the small party from his own crashed glider. Over there on the near horizon was the battle proper: or at least a third of it, that undertaken by General Gavin's 82nd U.S. Airborne Division.

Already the battle was in full swing. The invaders must have expected a stiff resistance and probably they could handle it, as most of their airborne troops had gone on unimpeded. But at that distance, there was no possible chance for a prisoner-observer to know whether the vital bridges had been blown or preserved.

Britwell paced up and down for a while. Occasionally, the trooper pushed open the door and looked in. His interest was fleeting, and a bored expression settled back on his full face as soon as he saw that all was well.

Going back over the earlier exchanges as he lay back on his bed, Britwell suddenly became aware that he had committed a blunder. He had called out the proper name of an Abwehr officer, Major Grunfeld, which he had only ever heard on the lips of Jan van Vliet. No wonder the bullying had ceased so quickly. None of them could have overlooked it. They knew that *he* knew more than a man in his position should.

Where would it lead? Britwell became nervous again, but they left him alone for three hours. When the summons came he was required to make himself ready for an immediate journey. Whither? Not to be evacuated for his own safety. To the Gestapo? Or to the H.Q. of some flinty-eyed field marshal with the plans for *Operation Market* spread out across his desk. *Grunfeld. Could he have heard the name when the major was telephoning?*

The jeep-type vehicle laid on for prisoner and escort journeyed eastward without benefit of lights.

6

The journey, which started soon after half past nine, promised to be a tedious one. Nothing had been said as to where they were heading but, clearly, Scoop had become a person of some importance and he was not to be left behind.

During the time when he was being interrogated in the cluster of cottages, the war correspondent had picked up a few details of local knowledge from the big map attached to a wall. He knew that the first incarceration point was in a small town called Vught: that Vught was perhaps two miles south of the Zuid Willemsvaart Canal which linked up with another town, 's-Hertogenbosch, on the regular road north which crossed the two rivers Maas and Waal and eventually went through Utrecht and Hilversum, on its way to Amsterdam and the Zuider Zee.

The corridor road selected by the allies for the advance north from the Belgian border was some ten miles to the east.

Ahead of the jeep, a single motor-cyclist acted as escort and guide. The major, the N.C.O. and guard seemed ill at ease, and no wonder, with a whole airborne army contesting the low-lying territory of Holland which their forces had occupied for so long.

As the gloom of night gathered around them, Britwell had plenty of time to look around. There were 'fireworks' in plenty, ranging from the south-east, through to due east and further north in the general direction of Nijmegen and Arnhem.

The prisoner's first surprise came when the motor-cyclist turned left down a narrow lane and led them abruptly to the canal, where a big flat-bottomed barge fully manned by German personnel at once took them aboard and ferried them across. On the other side, the barge guards lined up in two ranks and gave the salute as the major's vehicle rolled off and up the lane on the other side.

Sandwiched in the back between the *feldwebel* and the fat guard, Britwell felt anything but comfortable. After lowering his arm following the salute, the major glanced into the back. He grinned at Britwell in an engaging fashion and yawned to show that he was completely relaxed.

He said: 'We knew you were coming, Mr Britwell, even before you were so kind as to drop the plans for Operation Market Garden into our lap.'

The blunt announcement, partially muffled by the sound of the vehicle, took Britwell by surprise. Nevertheless, he thought he might learn something if he answered tactfully.

'How's that again, sir?'

'Perhaps your Government didn't tell you. Dummy parachutists were dropped as long ago as last Saturday. At a place called Emmerich, west of Utrecht. And there were others, east of Arnhem. I wonder how well you know your Holland? The R.A.F. attacked our barracks at certain key places shortly after noon on Sunday. We knew then that you were after the bridges. Some of our High Command were difficult to convince, but they are busy enough now.'

Britwell put on a bold face. 'Tell me, sir, are the key bridges still intact?'

After a pause, the major remarked: 'So far as I know they are still intact. The actual drops were a bit ragged. Already, supply drops are going awry. Further north, we are receiving British supplies and weapons. They come in handy to fight your countrymen with.'

'When do you think the war will end?'

The major sounded brusque. 'Who can tell? The British Government thought it might be over by Christmas, 1939, but it still goes on.'

Britwell could have argued that the British Government was being mis-quoted, but he refrained from saying anything and the conversation lapsed. In total darkness, occasionally brightened by the exploding of shells to the east, the tiny convoy kept moving steadily north-east at a modest pace.

In the last hour before midnight, a flight of allied bombers droned across the sky from west to east. Searchlights threw their moving cones of light across the sky, seeking and sometimes holding them and illuminating the falling bombs which rained down on the troops holding the vital corridor.

One of them suffered a direct hit. It turned turtle and returned losing height in the direction from which it had come, a smoking burning engine of war brightening the night sky until it exploded on impact far to the west.

Britwell was dozing between his guards when the jeep entered a small village, using a narrow lane on a down gradient. Two tall soldiers moved into their path with automatic weapons and a cowled torch. They looked over the occupants of the jeep while the motor-cyclist checked his machine beside the sentry hut.

The formalities were short-lived. On rolled the jeep, without the escort. The driver pulled up outside a large two-storey building with dormer windows protruding above the original roof. It looked like an old peacetime hotel converted into a wartime office block. Britwell was not far wrong in his surmise. In fact, it housed a cell of the Abwehr and was a key information centre with its own

German-manned radio system and telephone exchange.

More sentries flanked the steps which gave access to the darkened building. Britwell was left with his escort for a while, the major entering first and reporting to his superior. Hurrying booted feet came along the corridor. A junior officer beckoned them indoors, and the prisoner wondered once again if he was being officially turned over to the Gestapo.

The *feldwebel* disappeared through a door, and Britwell was left idling beside a table where an N.C.O. who acted as a sort of receptionist was seated. This man had plenty of writing to do, but he was willing enough to exchange a bit of excited gossip with the fat trooper when they were left alone.

On the wall opposite the table were two large portraits. One was a head and shoulders of the Fuhrer with his eyes glinting. His characteristic small moustache and quiff of hair seemed to be exaggerated. The other portrait was that of a man named Arthur Seyss-Inquart: an

Austrian who had thrown in his lot with the Third Reich early in 1939. After a careful vetting he had been given the office of commissioner of the Reich for the Netherlands.

Britwell would have liked a few minutes on his own with a sharp set of darts. He felt that he could improve the portrait of the Nazi maniac and the quisling, although darts was not his game.

A door on the right opened abruptly. The *feldwebel* escort came through it and clicked his heels. The fat trooper did the same, nudged Britwell into a more formal pose and prodded him towards the door. The prisoner was in for a few surprises; that was all too evident, but not the surprises he anticipated.

Firstly, there was the intense brightness of electric lighting everywhere. The big bustling room was like a goldfish bowl, specially illuminated for display. While the *feldwebel* was turning him over to a duty office guard, Britwell looked around. He was in a room big enough to be several knocked into one. Running some thirty feet down one side of it was a folding wooden partition with many glass panels above waist height. Through and beyond the partition were desks, filing cabinets, a big radio receiver and many German army personnel wearing headphones, or answering telephones and taking down messages.

Strolling up and down that room, deep in conversation, were the major who had brought him and an older man with broad shoulders, receding hair and an Iron Cross dangling across the front of his tunic supported by a ribbon worn round the neck.

These two were coming towards the partition as Britwell was hustled in, and they took the opportunity to study him at close quarters through the window glass. He did his best to return the compliment, although the new guard, bareheaded and alert, was moving him into a corner 'fenced off' by two long refectory tables which served as extra desks. Britwell was slow in sitting down on the upright wooden chair indicated for him. His eyes were busy.

He noted a few more details about the

senior officer and decided that he was still in the hands of the Abwehr, and not the Gestapo.

The clatter of typewriters from the other angle broke into his consciousness as he took in the officer's appearance. The head was long rather than square. The man was in his fifties. His neck, where his tunic fitted above the swinging Iron Cross, showed crinkled skin. The grey hair was thinning at the front, as Britwell had already noticed: it was also trimmed very close at the back and sides. Steel-rimmed spectacles magnified a pair of intense blue eyes which seemed to miss nothing.

The back of the upright chair nudged his spine: another thing he did not like about the Germans — assuming of course that it was German army issue. Again, the typewriters vied with the officers through the partition for his interest. He took note of another tall, hatless guard manning a door in the opposite wall to the one by which he had entered, and then his eyes were on the typists.

Female. Efficient and very busy. One of them a brunette: lean, flat-featured and with dark button eyes and a too-thin mouth. The other, taller, a year or so younger; long-necked in a graceful sort of way with a beautiful bell of hair, the colour of which he had heard described as titian. His heart did a backward somersault, while his observation went on. Titian. More like fine copper wire, especially the sheen on it. Freckles on the neck looked like healthy sunburn at that distance.

The women were seated around an alcove in the L-shaped room showing him their right profiles from an acute angle.

More heart thumping. A regular thumping beat like strident jungle jazz. In the old days, the auburn shoulder-length hair had usually hidden the back of the neck. Now, he noticed that it was tied back out of the way for business with a bright orange ribbon.

He said aloud: 'I don't believe it. This sort of luck just doesn't happen to me!'

The guards, facing one another on opposite sides of the room heard him but failed to comprehend his words. They exchanged pointed glances, arched their brows and awaited developments. The bespectacled officer drummed on the glass of the partition with his finger tips.

The typists, who had heard him do this before, both reacted, turning their heads and glancing towards him. Christina van Vliet's translucent blue eyes were arrested en route by the appearance of the latest prisoner to arrive, a man she had not yet scrutinised.

Britwell reacted almost as quickly. His racing thoughts were making him wonder how he looked to her. Without being actually aware of it, he had risen to his feet. Dressed as he was in battle-dress and a red beret on permanent loan from Micky Judd, he wondered how much he had startled her: if her nerves were bad: whether her presence here meant that she was still a prisoner, or whether she was on some sort of probation.

Christina coughed fitfully, pulled a white square of handkerchief out of a pocket in her black pleated skirt and hid her face in it. Having attracted their attention, the officer then pretended that he had tapped the partition unconsciously. He waved for them to get on with their work, but he seemed to have acquired some sort of satisfaction.

Still on his feet and feeling very conspicuous, Britwell picked up the chair and grounded it rather noisily. He rubbed his posterior and protested that a splinter of wood had entered his buttock. The nearer of the two guards went through the motions of examining the offending chair, but of course he found nothing. Behind Britwell's back, he touched his temple with a stubby forefinger, and the whole room settled back to routine.

Britwell, who was not a nail-biter, pretended that he was for a while. It was after midnight. The personnel he had seen so far all looked as if they had been on duty all day. He wondered if the women would be given a spell off, or whether the witching hour was set aside for interrogating over-tired too-dumb prisoners.

He *was* over-tired, but the discovery of Christina working at a typewriter at his second port of call in Holland had given him a boost which nothing could counteract. Or so he thought, as he cogitated over the series of dastardly tricks which fate had played upon him since he had moved disspiritedly into Paris half a lifetime ago with the Civil Affairs team.

He thought: Hell! One thing I'm sure of. I'm hooked on this girl as far as the emotions are concerned.

The two typewriters stopped almost at the same time. The typists were still busy, however, checking over their recent work. The two officers opened the door in the partition and came through. In the other part of the room a relieving team of radio-operators, cipher clerks and tele-phonists took over from the retiring watch.

Britwell blinked as the two officers came before him, only separated from him by one of the wooden tables. The voice of the senior officer had a deceptive silky quality about it, as though he were caressing the English language.

'Mr Britwell, I believe. Major Grunfeld

has told me of your er, recent misfortunes. I hope you are not the worrying kind, Mr Britwell. I put it to you, however, that if your glider had gone all the way to the intended dropping zone you might have been dead now.'

Something in the manner of this officer induced Scoop to show him a little respect. As soon as he was spoken to, he rose to his feet, came to attention, but did not salute.

'I try not to worry, Herr — '

The speaker brought his hands from behind his back. He pushed his spectacles higher up his nose, gestured for Britwell to be at ease, and resumed. 'Forgive me, I did not introduce myself. Colonel Fritz Gerhardt of the Abwehr III F. This has been a very busy day for us. Soon, we shall be sending our typists home. You will be shown a room in another part of the hotel. This is the busiest day we have had for some time. I wouldn't think of asking you any more questions before you have had the time to rest. Excuse us, please.'

Britwell bent from the hips in a

half-bow. They turned away and continued out of the room by the door opposite. A telephone rang on the typists' desk. The brunette put aside the work of both of them which she had been sorting and answered it. The conversation was short and to the point. She hung up, yawned and forced a tight smile for Christina's benefit and moved off through the partition with the typed papers.

The door by which Britwell had entered was then locked by the guard, who crossed over to his opposite number, glanced around and then stepped with him through the other door. Christina had reached her outdoor clothes from one of two rough wooden pegs let into the wall above her desk. They consisted of a track suit: trousers and a buttoned long-sleeved blouse almost like battle-dress. The material was a coarse brown colour. Stitched to the front and back of the blouse were two circles of orange material, the sort which showed up in the dark. The one on the front was in two halves until the garment was buttoned up.

As she dressed herself for outdoors, the

girl whispered: 'Harry, it *is* you? There are thousands of things I would like to say to you but there isn't time. You're a prisoner, no?'

'Yes, Christina. Are you — a prisoner?'

'Well, not exactly. Let's say I'm under surveillance, eh? I'm allowed to run to my lodgings, and sometimes I take messages to our people. It's risky, of course, but I feel I have to do it. I was thinking of contacting some of my Dutch friends tonight. All is far from well with the British further north, in the region of Arnhem. But your arrival changes things. Maybe I can get the Resistance to get you out of here. At least, I can try.'

'It's nice to know you care, Christina, after all this time. But I wouldn't want you to fall under suspicion again. I'd rather stay a prisoner, or try to get out on my own.'

The girl smiled nervously as she changed her day shoes for a pair of plimsolls. 'Why — why are you here, an' not further north with your own people?'

'It's a long story, my dear. If I told you I came to Holland because of you, after talking with Marie and Jan in Paris, you wouldn't believe me. But it is true. As for my arriving here when I thought you were possibly in Dreibergen, that was pure chance. My glider was brought down too soon. I was captured near Vught and brought here by Major Grunfeld. I don't know what they plan for me, but they may suspect that we know each other. So, be careful. I shan't be able to sleep if I know you're taking risks.'

Christina chuckled. 'Lovely to see you again, but in a way I wish you hadn't come. I'm frightened for you now. That changes things.'

Before they could say more, the other typist, a German national, came back through the partition and started chatting easily with the Dutch girl. Britwell found himself ignored. He wondered if this little conversation had been engineered by the Abwehr, whether it had been possible for them to be overheard.

He nodded curtly as the two women left together. Shortly afterwards, one of the guards came back and escorted him to one of two attics at the top of the building. The room was bare, except for the sheer necessities. The dormer window was barred and blacked out.

Britwell was settling down under two loaned blankets on the single bed when Major Grunfeld strolled in, smoking a cigarette through an amber holder. In spite of the hour, he seemed in a jovial mood.

'I see there's still plenty of activity over Grave to the east,' he remarked, glancing through the blackout. 'Here in Zuidmaas, things will stay quiet for a while. I reckon that by now the Dutch girl, van Vliet, will have trotted back to her lodgings. An interesting family, the van Vliets. She wanted to run in the 1940 Olympics, but that one was cancelled and now the 1944. What a shame! But I let her keep in training. What harm can it do?'

Britwell was troubled by the major's observations, but he merely nodded and smiled and did not attempt to reply. Presently, the Abwehr man, noting his mood, withdrew and put out the light. Some light still penetrated through a skylight over the door. Grunfeld exchanged a few words with the guard posted in the narrow passage between the attics.

There was a joke about the Englishman getting it first if the Allies decided to bomb the building in what remained of the night. Perhaps an hour later, Britwell dropped off into a troubled sleep, his whole body yearning for Christina.

7

There was no need for a dawn chorus of birds to rouse the non-Dutch intruders in the small town of Zuidmaas. Before six o'clock the resounding noises of renewed battle came from the east, where General Jim Gavin's sky troops were fighting along the middle sector of the vital corridor which was the airborne army's chief objective.

British and American fighters and bombers went over the area and systematically bombed and strafed the main German fortified points in a valiant attempt to assist the grounded fighting men. Nearer, German flak batteries contested the allied air forces' right to be in the sky over Holland.

Britwell came up out of a shallow sleep, crossed to the window and drew the blinds. His view was to the north. By standing on tiptoe he could see beyond the rooftops where the Maas river split the countryside. Large orange flags flying from bedroom windows lifted his spirits a little. This far, he had not seen much of the local population.

Still straining for height he saw a milk man with a horse and cart making his deliveries with an orange arm band proudly displayed over his white jacket. In front of the building, military vehicles came and went as the German war machine moved smoothly but with haste to cope with the emergencies which the sudden sky attack had thrust upon them.

He dressed quickly, washed himself without benefit of soap at the small wash basin fitted into a corner of the room. His face was hidden in the towel when an unfamiliar German guard unlocked the door and cautiously stepped inside with a tray containing his breakfast. He lifted the lid of the coffee pot, sniffed the pleasant aroma and turned his attention to the small rolls and croissants. There was a small pat of butter and a tiny jar of jam which looked like plum.

He grinned and thanked the guard and started to eat as soon as the fellow had withdrawn his bulk from the room. His thoughts were busy. Some of the major's revelations of the night before were very likely the truth. If the German ground forces had been waiting for a sky drop it was possible that they had so harassed the parachutists and the glider troops that the invaders had been ousted from their planned ground positions.

What Britwell did not know at that time, nor was likely to know for a day or two, was that the British dropping zones were several miles from Arnhem and the vital bridges in the town. It had been thought by the planners that the open ground nearer to the Arnhem sector was too soft, too muddy for landings. It was known to be polderland, land reclaimed from the sea, and as such it was suspect for gliders and the assembling of light vehicles and guns.

He brooded over the possible fate of his countrymen as he cleared the tray of eatables. As soon as he had finished, he started to pace the floor. He had two, or possibly three separate problems now. Firstly, the plight of the British further north. On that point, he felt that he ought to be there, although his own physical presence, that of one man supposed to be a non-combatant, could not make much difference.

Secondly, there was Christina: her future and her immediate safety meant a whole lot to him. He admitted to himself that he had been motivated by his heart when he made his last stubborn effort to get into Holland, following the chance meeting with her brother and Marie Smith in Paris. Thirdly, and it was still worth considering: his own safety. As a prisoner of the Abwehr almost anything could happen to him. He had already noted that the senior officers of the counter-intelligence corps were very mobile. They might decide to move their personnel again and take him with them. Or, if they lost interest in him, he could be shipped to the Third Reich to await the arrival of the victorious allies in some down-town prison or cell block.

Ten minutes later, his dirty dishes were removed by the same guard. Next, he received a visit from a fair-haired fanatical-looking *feldwebel* about thirty years of age who announced that the major was allowing him to take some exercise in the compound at the rear of the hotel.

Britwell thanked him, and went off down the stairs between the N.C.O. and a trooper. Unfortunately, the route they took did not give him a chance to look in the room where Christina worked. On that score, he had to take a grip on his patience.

Monday, September 18th was a fine day. Fine for supply drops and offensive sorties by air against the Germans in Holland. But was the weather sufficient of an advantage to put things right in the area of Arnhem?

In the rear courtyard, he looked about with interest. There was a stone wall, six feet in height completely enclosing the exercise area behind the building. Beyond it, with trees in between was a row of houses. A man smoking a clay pipe caught a glimpse of him from an upper window as he walked towards the outer wall.

From time to time, in his strolling, Britwell pulled up near the big eight-feet wide gate in the rear wall. It had been filled in so that it was solid. Each time he went near it, one of the two armed guards had a mild attack of nerves, as though he was planning to make a break for freedom.

Every now and then, the voices of Dutch housewives, calling cheerfully to one another as they hurried over the essential shopping, carried to the prisoner. There were many bikes about, and an occasional horse and cart.

Britwell allowed his wanderings to slow down, as though his legs were tired. Eventually, he sat down with his back to the wall which gave onto the street and whistled one or two catchy tunes which had been popular in England at the time he left. All the time his eyes were busy behind his sunglasses, staring fitfully into the busy operations room, while he strove to give the impression that his mind was blank and his interest on the sky, and the birds busy around the ivy-clad eaves.

Presently, he heard a smoker's cough

on the other side of the wall. It came at a time when the guard who favoured the gate had moved to the other end of the building to chat with his opposite number. Britwell whistled and stopped, whistled and stopped. And waited.

'Is it all right to talk, Englishman?'

'Yes, if you keep your voice down, friend. What can I do for you?'

The old man chuckled. 'It is good to know the allies are here, but they have taken on a lot of trouble. My folks tell me I'm a pessimist, but we could have waited till the ground troops came up from Belgium. How long will it take for them to get here, do you think?'

'Mijnheer, I'm not Winston Churchill. I wouldn't know. Perhaps just a few weeks more. A lot depends on the bridges. Advancing troops have to cross rivers to make headway in the act of liberation.'

Having dropped his head on his chest as though he was dozing, Britwell murmured without fear of being over-heard.

'Aye, aye, the bridges. You've said it. That's what you came for, wasn't it? To safeguard the bridges. I hope your folks manage it, but the rumours from the north don't sound too good for the British. Most of the troops seem to be held up outside Arnhem, and there's talk of panzers being rushed this way from Gelderland. Tanks that were supposed to be permanently out of action. I hope the British general knows about them.'

Britwell felt depressed. 'I suppose the Resistance will be in touch with them by radio. The Dutch will help all they can.'

'I'm sure you're right, but the groups north of here are so closely watched they can hardly make a move. A man told me the British radios don't have a big enough range. But I don't want to depress you.'

The informer made a sharp hissing noise, as a warning, murmured that he would have to clear out. Britwell took this as his cue to take a stroll. During a similar stroll in the afternoon, he managed to locate himself behind a bit of stunted wicker fencing near an open window in the operations room.

Grunfeld's voice on the telephone carried to him. ' . . . the van Vliet girl? I think we watched her too closely last night. We'll give her another run tonight. Send her home early. If our men happen to lose her it might be as well to try the Kees Schenk house. I'm sure she doesn't know what's happened there. Yes. Yes, we'll keep in touch, Colonel. Auf wiedersehen.'

Britwell recoiled rather than withdrew to a greater distance. During the rest of his 'liberty' he sought and longed for an opportunity to contact his Dutch girl friend, but nothing came of it.

★   ★   ★

That evening Major Grunfeld himself dismissed Christina van Vliet just a few minutes after nine o'clock. She took this early dismissal with mixed feelings, although she tried not to show them. Grunfeld stayed in the room while she changed, showing an interest in her attitude rather than her comely athlete's figure.

He said: 'You have slight marks under your eyes as though you are not sleeping well. You must take care. Keep up your training. If the plimsolls wear too thin, let me know. I may be able to get you a new pair.'

With an outsize effort, she flashed him her most disarming smile. After thanking him for his continued kindness in trying times, she said a farewell to her fellow typist and left the building. All the guards in the front of the hotel watched her run off with her long loping stride.

As soon as she was out of sight, she slowed down to a walk and gave herself over to the thoughts which had been troubling her all day. They had watched her the night before. The special guards hidden in the bushes, at corners, looking for Dutch nationals who broke the curfew. Their widespread presence had unnerved her, so that she did not dare approach anyone connected with the Resistance in case she brought trouble to them. But time was passing, and the Abwehr treatment of Harry Britwell might change swiftly for the worse. This far, he was still at the Zuidmaas Hotel. What if they whipped him away without

115

any warning? He could be inside the Reich in not much more than an hour. If that happened, there was no guaranteeing he would survive the war.

She knew that her brother, Jan, had made some sort of a deal with Abwehr III F, otherwise she would not have been liberated at the beginning of the month. What if they planned to use Harry Britwell as well as Jan? Her thoughts became confused by worry.

She returned to her lodgings, washed and changed and ate a light meal prepared tastefully by her landlady who always complained about the lack of variety in food commodities, even though her husband kept a grocer's shop. Mevrouw Nottet sniffed when Christina began to put on her track suit again. She had no inclination towards physical fitness and the outdoor life.

'You'll have rheumatism in all your joints before you're *my* age girl, if you keep on trotting everywhere like a young foal. You'll see!'

Christina turned and waved. She had a feeling that she might never live to see

Mevrouw Nottet's age, the way things were going for the van Vliets. The house was to the south-east of town. Christina trotted first towards the north. Her progress was noted by a trooper sitting silently on a gravestone in the cemetery. He waved, and she called a greeting. Down to the riverside she went. She sat for a few moments on a built out platform dangling her feet above the water.

She was making plans and waiting for the darkness to thicken. Another trooper stopped watching the eastern 'fireworks' and saw her running away again. She took no thought of hiding her movements until she had passed the man in the cemetery. After that, she showed stealth. First, she used her fine leg muscles to vault over a low wall. Hidden in a backyard, she stripped off the track suit top with the bright give-away orange circles on it and deliberately turned it inside out.

Next, she removed the ribbon from her hair. With her face lightly blacked over with soot, she continued on her way: towards the south-west corner of the town. Two German cyclists on creaking bicycles missed her as she took shelter, and then she had to wait on a corner until a watchful pair in a narrow alley finished their cigarettes and their hourly chitchat.

The last fifty yards, she was as invisible as a cat on the prowl. With a quick athletic leap she cleared the low wall at the back of Kees Schenk's house and tapped a pattern of sound on the pane of the kitchen window. To her surprise, nothing happened. She listened hard but never detected any sort of sound from within.

Her next move was to find two bricks low in the rear wall where a key was hidden against emergencies. It took a long time to probe the gap and when she managed to do so with a twig from the narrow garden she had no luck. The key had gone. The house was empty. No means of access. She started to think hard, although she was troubled. The railway strike must have accounted for it. Kees worked for the Dutch national railway system. A general strike had been called on the Sunday in an effort to help the Allies with their air armada. There was a sound enough reason for the Schenks to have withdrawn. No need to panic. But what should she do now? Who should she contact to help with Harry?

In the short time she had been in Zuidmaas, she had not really had the chance to make many acquaintances. Her knowledge of the *onderduikers* in the area was limited, and she was shrewd enough to know that many of them would hesitate to trust her, seeing that she had been brought into their midst by the Abwehr.

However, she did know one location: one point of contact. A disused warehouse down by the river. Near the western extremity of the town. It was roofless, with a basement not known to the Germans. This much she knew through listening hard in her lodgings. Thither she must go, to make her plea for help.

On the way, she took fifteen minutes. She dodged one cycle patrolman by lying full length along the top of a high wall until he was out of sight. Another one, rendered suspicious by seeing her fleeting shadow, had to be put off by tossing small stones for him to investigate.

At last, she reached the deserted wharf. It looked dark, damp, lonely and unfriendly, but she was not to be put off. After testing the darkness, she slipped over the wooden extension to the stone banking, and levered herself along it hanging by her arms. Within half a minute she was close enough to drum a contact message with the toe of her plimsoll against the stout wooden wall of the basement.

Instantly, there was a dull thud from beyond. Seconds later, the return message was tapped out. Breathing quietly through her mouth, Christina muscled herself up again, wriggled a few yards and then negotiated her entry to the roofless building through a window which was reduced to a gaping hole. Again, her legs made light of the exertion. She crossed to a big trapdoor with a rusting ring through it and dropped almost soundlessly, full length beside it. A tiny gap of light appeared between the planks, not wider than a centimetre. She was newly aware of her hair cascading around her face and neck. Perhaps she had been foolish to run with it swinging loose. She felt inside her tunic, produced a black beret and began stuffing her hair into it.

'Who is there?'

'Christina van Vliet. I want help.'

A short pause for consultation. It did not appear to take long.

'We cannot help you tonight. Go away. Mind how you go. You are risking a lot.'

'No. No, listen to me first. I *won't* go.' Some of the pigheadedness which Jan was supposed to have more of his fair share of came to the fore in the whispered argument. Another pause. No change in the tone of voice. Still the same man. Toneless, indescribable.

'What is it you want? Hurry it up!'

'The Englishman held at the hotel. Harry Britwell. The Abwehr have plans for him. He has to be freed before they lose their patience.'

'We know of him. He is not even a soldier. Leave him be. We have more important matters to deal with. Now, clear off, you hear?'

121

Christina clenched her fists, but this time she did not argue. 'If not tonight, when?'

'Who can say? You are working against our best interests. Go!'

Reluctantly, she rose to her feet. She felt sad, defeated: drained of stamina, which was unusual for her. It was the baying of the hound which gave her the first warning that all was not well. No sooner had she started to think that it might be following her scent than her intuition confirmed it. Someone at the hotel, probably the major, had given an article of her clothing to those who sought her. Somehow, the animal had succeeded in tracing her when the humans had failed. But this was a real emergency.

She went back to the trapdoor, and talked through it in a heated whisper for several seconds. Not waiting for confirmation from below, she dictated the plans.

'They're from the recreation hall, I believe. A dozen or more. I'm going to lead them right back in here, where I'm standing. You will tackle them from the sides. I shall go via the river. No survivors, mind, and get that dog!'

So saying she moved away. As soon as she was through the window, she released her hair again and rapidly turned her tunic inside out so that the bright orange circles were visible. She thought: I'm getting myself and others into a fix, Harry, my love, but all is not lost yet. Maybe I'll win support for your cause!

Two men being hauled along by the outsize dog; flashing torches and calling to others as though secrecy did not matter any more, on account of the river was close and no one, not even a class runner could go much further than that.

Ten men in the warehouse basement rapidly adjusted to the new situation. When Christina arrived they had been on the point of leaving to make a raid on that self-same building, the town community centre which had been taken over and used as a recreation hall for German personnel.

Christina ran into the road, towards the two troopers with the dog. Promptly, they saw her and pointed. One of them shouted 'Halte!' but she took no notice, merely pausing in her tracks and racing back towards the warehouse. Another six troopers followed the first pair. There was a lot more shouting, but no one thought of firing a burst after the retreating figure.

Breathing hard, she launched herself through the black square opening which was the window and landed neatly in a forward roll on the rough flooring. There were specific sounds beneath her now as the Dutchmen gathered for action. At either end of the basement, there were metal ladders rising vertically up the sides and the walls of the roofless upper structure. Two key men came out of the lower room and started up the ladders with light machine-guns slung over their shoulders.

The Germans were still some yards away when the hound was released. Growling savagely, it bounded forward, sniffed at the window and clumsily leapt up to the sill and scrambled inside. At the same time, Christina — her heart thumping with excitement — did a running dive through a window space at the other end into the river.

The water skills she had learned as a girl in her middle teens served her well. She rose to the surface, breathing hard, got her bearings and started upstream using a powerful crawl stroke. Her direction gradually brought her closer to the south bank from which she had started.

Fortunately, the hound was not as courageous in water as on land. Instead of leaping out through the window Christina had used, it contented itself in barking hard and resting its forepaws on the sill.

The first trooper to reach the window peered in cautiously. He found his voice and exhorted the dog to do its duty. Shoulders, boots and rifle butts pounded on the door until it splintered and fell inwards. All but two of the eight Germans went through it in a close group. They were taken completely by surprise when the Dutch machine-gunners opened up on them from the windows on either side.

Four struggling troopers went down in the first burst of crossfire. The other two were mown down when the trapdoor came up and two belching Spandaus pumped bullets at them. German weapons and ammunition used against Germans.

Three Dutchmen raced across the floor and, aided by a spot of luck, were able to cut down the two remaining troopers by firing lethal bursts from the windows and door. A brief extra burst finished off the dog. Its body was unceremoniously bundled into the river.

There was a pause while the weapons of the hapless Germans were collected. No one bothered about Christina's progress. The Resistance men knew that they would have to move out of the area before dawn. The small town would be too hot to hold them after this bold strike.

The alarm hooters were sounding. A jeep and motor-cycles were headed for the river as Christina hauled herself out upstream, and headed back to her lodgings, making use of gardens, basements and every scrap of cover. Mevrouw Nottet was waiting for her at the kitchen door, her nervous hands clutching her shawl across her puny chest.

'Good gracious, girl, what have you been up to *this* time? Swimming, is it? Get yourself up to the bathroom. Take a bath. You'll catch your death of cold. Leave that — that running suit with me. I'll wash it out and dry it quickly. Off you go now. Up with you!'

Christina gave the woman a light hug, and begged her to go off to bed as soon as the track suit was drying in front of the fire.

Feeling guilty about her own superb health, the auburn-haired girl quietly soaked herself in a warm bath and rubbed herself down with a big bath towel. She knew from creaking floorboards that most of the occupants of the house had been awakened by the shooting and rushing about; none of them, however, would come out asking questions in case they had to face formidable cross-examinations later.

As she shrugged down into her single bed, Christina's guilty feelings about forcing the local Resistance men out into the open gradually subsided. They knew what they were up against, and they would expect to move on again. Their withdrawal might ensure that there would be no reprisals against the town population.

What sort of a reception would she get when she returned to the Zuidmaas Hotel for work in the morning? she wondered. And what of Harry Britwell? The events of the night might very well prompt the Abwehr to move him out of town.

Troubling thoughts. Nevertheless, she attempted to sleep for an hour or two.

8

The Zuidmaas Hotel, meanwhile, was the focal point of a great deal of activity. What had started out as a simple operation, tailing a young Dutch girl to see where she would run to, and whether she would attempt to deceive those who were watching her, had developed into a minor emergency.

There were no more than two score troops in the town at nightfall. Many of them were Abwehr personnel, and the rest had been recuperating from illnesses or slight wounds sustained around the time of the sky drop.

Christina van Vliet was forgotten as Major Grunfeld hastily dressed in the villa near the hotel and hurried back to his place of duty to find out what had happened down by the river. He drove down to the scene of the action in his jeep with a feldwebel and two troopers. There, he found a young lieutenant and perhaps a dozen troopers scouring the south bank on either side of the warehouse for the Resistance fighters who had wiped out no less than eight of their number.

Grunfeld identified the bodies of two of his men, those who had taken the hound along with them. He questioned the junior officer who had little information of any real value, and then returned to the hotel, having decided to leave the operation in the hands of the Wehrmacht.

At the hotel, he ran a check at all levels, spoke by telephone to Colonel Gerhardt who was in the next town and reluctantly agreed to spend the rest of the evening in the hotel, in case the Dutch Resistance fighters decided to make another strike before daylight.

In his attic on the north side, Harry Britwell was just as uneasy. The distant gunfire had roused him. He wondered at first if this was some sort of a diversion to get German troops away from the hotel prior to making an attack on the building. The more he thought about it, however, the more it seemed unlikely. Why should Resistance fighters risk their lives for one solitary British non-combatant on the say-so of a single Dutch girl from out of town?

He lay on his bed with his hands behind his head and thought what was best to be done. Any sort of lone sortie would be fraught with danger, but he ought to make an effort unaided on his own behalf so as not to have Christina and the patriots risk their lives on a fool's errand.

Even though it seemed unlikely, there was still a chance they might attack the hotel. What could he do, though, to change things? His mind was dull with too much conjecture when the familiar drone of aircraft came from the west.

Air raid alarms sounded on the outskirts of the town, alerting isolated guns' crews for possible action. He slipped out of bed, prowled around barefooted in his underwear and listened at the door. The upper storey had gone quiet since the earlier spot check on all rooms. Through the door, he could hear the light snoring of the man left on guard in the narrow passage between the attics.

That and the aircraft passing overhead drove him to take risks.

He switched on the attic light, tiptoed over to his window and cautiously opened the blackout curtain. It was good to see the high-flying bombers going across the sky with the probing searchlights seeking to illuminate them and pin them down. There was no reaction to what he was doing from the courtyard down below.

It occurred to him that he was acting rather stupidly in trying to attract bombers, the pilots of which had already been briefed as to their targets. He ought to be trying to slip past the guard, or doing something more positive. What, he did not know.

His folded daywear clothes were in a neat heap on the floor by the end of the bed. Should he risk dressing, in case an opportunity to slip out came along?

He was sufficiently mature to know that Christina's vulnerability was bugging him, that he was not thinking clearly enough to do anything positive and worthwhile. Nevertheless, something *had* to be done. The drone of the planes was fading now. He crossed to the window and put the drapes back in place. Next, he moved over to the clothes. He was stooping over them when the surprise came.

Schulz, the guard in the passage, was still snoring lightly as a key turned in the lock and Erich Adler, the fair *feldwebel* with the wild look in his eyes, bounded into the room. One glance at the bent-over figure was sufficient. As Britwell straightened up, Adler clouted him on the side of the jaw with the butt of his machine-pistol.

Pain screwed up the neutral-coloured eyes in the lean, sun darkened features. Britwell reeled back. He could have rolled aside and fought off the attack of nausea which possessed him, but it occurred to him that this was not an occasion for a show of bravery.

He sank back against the foot of the bed, rolled over with an arm half raised to protect himself and slowly slumped on the floor, face downwards and apparently unconscious.

Adler called: 'Schulz, get yourself in

here.' That much Britwell fully understood. Some of the exchanges which followed, however, went right over his head. No other German appeared and the incident seemed as if it would remain a minor key one between Schulz and Adler.

Adler was cursing and berating the other. He was saying that Schulz was behaving like he used to do as a boy, sleeping in his father's hay loft instead of seeing to the animals. The *feldwebel* explained about the light being on, and how the blackout curtain had been pulled aside to attract the attention of the R.A.F.

Schulz grovelled and Adler gave it to him again. By sheer luck, he explained, no one else had noticed the light on and the blackout being moved: but it was a wonder, seeing that the major could not sleep, lower down in the building.

Adler, thumping up and down the attic in his soft-soled shoes, said that if they weren't second cousins, if they hadn't grown up together in the same village, he would have reported Schulz to the major without hesitation. As it was, Schulz was getting off with a caution from his immediate superior, Adler.

The *feldwebel* concluded: 'Are you wide awake now?'

Schulz swore he was. He removed Britwell's clothing, on orders and followed his 'townie' to the top of the stairs, still thanking him effusively in a low voice. Left in the dark, Britwell wondered whether to recover, or leave it a while.

Schulz bustled in again, knelt on one knee and turned him over. Assuming that his prisoner was still far from conscious the shaken guard hoisted him up and dumped him roughly on the bed. Having done this, the trooper withdrew and began to pace the corridor with a steady tread.

Back among his blankets, Britwell had plenty of time to reflect on the simple but brilliant tactic of removing a man's clothes to make him ineffective. He spent a minute or two gently fingering the line of his jaw where the butt of the Schmeisser had connected.

There was a definite swelling there, but it might have been much bigger. Perhaps the fair stubble along the jawline (a few shades darker than his cranial hair, sun-bleached in two continents) had protected the flesh.

No clothes . . . one stage worse off than before he made his abortive effort with the blackout. But for one thing, which made him smile broadly, in spite of the pain along his lower jaw. Schulz had forgotten to turn the key in the lock. Surely not? Britwell went back over the incident, every little detail being clear to him due to the shock of being suddenly apprehended.

He felt sure that he was right. Schulz had done the unpardonable thing: left the door undone. Even so, nothing would happen unless the oversight was taken advantage of. Assuming the British battle-dress stuff was nowhere around, did Britwell feel sufficiently desperate to 'jump' Schulz and acquire his trooper's outfit?

If and when he took advantage of Trooper Schulz, the other floors had to be negotiated. If he was noticed wearing the trooper's uniform there was more than an even chance he would be shot out of hand. Britwell sighed. The early hours of the morning was a time when his initiative was at its lowest. He had a feeling that troops in a town which had already been shaken by sudden gunfire would fire at shadows.

If he stayed, he might be the unwilling guest of the Abwehr indefinitely, with free travel nearer and nearer to Berlin . . .

Nevertheless, the unlocked door presented an opportunity of sorts. It was a challenge. Something to think about, and maybe — just maybe — to act upon.

★　★　★

The internal alarm buzzer sounded in the Zuidmaas Hotel almost exactly on 0300 hours. It came within a minute of the earlier air raid warning signals beyond the building occasioned by yet another intrusion by allied aircraft, and this time, seemingly, looking for a target in Zuidmaas instead of further east.

No one in the building ever knew whether the director of bombing operations in the Home Counties had received specific knowledge as to the location of a German communications centre in Zuid-maas, or whether the raid on the small town was just to keep the German army of occupation on its toes.

Schulz moved to the telephone located where the top stairs and corridor joined. He lifted the receiver, prepared to obey hasty instructions to evacuate the top storey. Such was not the case.

'Schulz, this is Adler, here. At the present moment, we are evacuating all personnel off the main floor into the basement. It is not on account of the air raid. I repeat, this is not on account of the air raid. You are to stay put right where you are. Those are the major's orders. If you hear hostile shots being fired down below, don't panic. Have you heard all right?'

Schulz, a tall, thick-set countryman in his late twenties with a brooding expression and a permanently blue-black chin, wanted to ask many questions, but after his previous brush with authority he dared not prolong the telephone call. It did not occur to him straight away that the major's personnel had withdrawn into the basement so as to be in a position to inflict shocking casualties on any Resistance unit reckless enough to attack and enter the building.

Schulz put down the receiver and was at once jumped from behind by Britwell who had been prodded into action by the air raid warning signals and the insistent buzzing of the internal warning system.

Britwell hit him hard at the side of his neck with the base of his right palm. This thrust his head into the wall and made him gasp. Schulz's helmet, substituted for his forage cap at the time of the alarm, banged against the wall and left his head. Britwell caught it and hit him with it as he squirmed about and clutched for the barrel of his discarded machine-pistol.

Dodging a knee and then a boot, Britwell moved his under-clad body with all the dexterity he possessed. Schulz's bobbing Adam's apple seemed awfully close as the prisoner aimed a sharp down chop with the side of his left hand. The blow was aimed for the side of the neck but due to the shifting of the target it landed further forward, partially over the windpipe with devastating result.

Schulz gasped for breath. His eyes seemed more prominent as the battle for air took precedence over the man to man struggle. While the German sagged against the wall, Britwell picked up the machine pistol and assumed command.

The guard staggered, rather than walked into the attic. After checking the stairs, the war correspondent moved in after him and closed the door.

'Now, Schulz, if you want to see the Fatherland again — I mean the Third Reich, do as you're told. Schnell! Undress!'

Very gradually, Schulz's breathing improved, but he was slow to comply with Britwell's demands; so much so that the angry prisoner dealt him a hard blow in the stomach with the muzzle of the automatic weapon. Schulz coughed as more breath was forced out of him, but this time he did make a definite effort to get out of his clothes.

Britwell trussed his hands and feet with strips of cloth ripped from bed sheets with the new prisoner's bayonet. Another strip pulled the stockinged feet well up the back towards the trussed hands. For extra measure, a handkerchief was thrust into the gasping mouth and kept in place with another length of cotton sheeting.

Uncomfortably aware of his prisoner's close regard from the bed, Britwell struggled into the trousers and the boots. He was fortunate in finding the footwear almost exactly the same size as his own. He slowed up as he turned his attention to the tunic. Not because he did not want to be on his way. It was largely because he did not relish the tricky business of getting out of the building.

The peculiar whistle of falling bombs broke in upon his concentration and made him wonder speculatively just how far away the explosions would be. He had no idea, of course, that the floor below had been vacated.

Two bombs landed first. One across the river, in open land, and the other in the river itself. Two more bracketed the town east and west: others were to follow. The staccato crackle of long lean-muzzled anti-aircraft guns heightened the general crescendo.

Britwell pushed the forage cap on his head and crossed with the keys to the other attic. He was in there, flashing a torch over the empty bed and other meagre facilities when the next stick of bombs came whining down. He tried to think himself into the mood for a big effort. If he was going to bluff his way out of the building, it had to be done quite soon. Before the next personnel check, for instance, or any change of guards.

He counted until he thought that the bombs would have landed. Still no concussion. Seconds built up. The beginnings of panic in the mind, and then the devastating double explosion of projectiles erupting within just a few yards of each other.

Brilliant flashes of orange and white light penetrated the thick blackout material over the window. The terrific vibrations and the all-consuming noise of the twin explosions seemed to come next. It could not have been so, but Britwell always thought that the glancing blow against the eastern end of the building came later.

Beyond the attic door, the rest of the upper storey seemed to be blown apart. This was his chance, his one in a thousand opportunity, and yet he could not take it straight away on account of his ears were singing like those of a man drowning at great depth. His eyes felt as if they were giving out sparks of light. His whole body was shaken. And yet the brain functioned.

Beams, tiles, plaster and stonework were still moving in a fine haze of dust as he opened the door, prepared for the worst. The ceiling below had collapsed, so that he could see in patches all the way through to the operations room. Stepping gingerly across to the other attic, he found that the bed had gone through and poor Schulz with it. So had a greater part of the end wall.

Oddly enough, his sun spectacles were still lying on the narrow shelf under the mirror where he would have liked to shave, given the chance. He gathered them up, returned to the other room and was in time to witness the falling out of the window glass due to spreading pressures around the roof.

He stuck his head out rather gingerly, and became aware of a drainpipe running all the way down to the ground. Did he have the nerve to use it? There was a crater in the road just twenty yards away. No one so far had emerged from below to ascertain the extent of the damage.

While he hesitated, someone below buzzed the corridor telephone. That did it. There was life down below: someone would be up to investigate quite soon. Licking his dry lips, he swung the Schmeisser over his shoulder by the strap, grabbed for the pipe and hung on. It held him, although not very far away there were still subsidences taking place.

He started to go down, the boots of his borrowed footwear firmly planted against the wall. On one occasion, the fore part of his helmet brushed the wall. He had no recollection of putting it on his head before beginning the descent, but no matter. Hand over hand, without benefit of glove protection he worked his way down the pipe.

Out of his eye corner, he was aware of the ops room going by. It seemed to take an age. And then, as the dust and debris were about settled, a section of someone's garden wall decided to cant slowly and with dignity into the newly-formed crater. The sheer incongruity of this unexpected development affected Scoop's concentration. One hand slipped.

He grazed the other, stubbed his knee against the wall, and suddenly fell the last ten feet to the ground. Unconsciously, he acted according to that rigorous training he had received in the parachute school. Feet and knees together, and the special sort of roll they had taught him. He did it all, and reasonably well. Later, he was to feel bruises on his back where new sharp debris had dug into it, but to a man escaping that was a small price to pay.

Instinct told him to skirt the town on the east side and make for the polderland further south. He did so, finding his way unerringly in a matter of some fifteen minutes. As his tired feet cleared the last of the buildings, he wondered if he would ever know the identity of the bomb aimer who had hit the hotel at a time vital to his escape.

9

A puzzling thought struck Britwell as he staggered onto the beginnings of the lowland soil which had been reclaimed by the determined efforts of the Dutch in the pre-war era. He was baffled about the invisibility of the local population: particularly children. There were so few of them about that one could almost imagine a sort of wartime Pied Piper having enticed them into a cavern in some great hillside.

Except that there were very few hillsides in that part of Holland. A bit of inspired guesswork produced the true answer. The families were spending a lot of their time in the cellars and basements. After all, the war had been going on for years now: the Dutch knew how to look after their own.

He estimated that dawn was less than half an hour away as he stumbled over heavy turfed land beyond a narrow wooden fence. A mist had formed up along the polder, lowering the temperature and making breathing a relatively unpleasant thing to do.

He had learned little about the polder when he was brought north by jeep and, in the present circumstances, he did not want to go very far from town until daylight came. He had a feeling he might find himself isolated in the middle of low-lying land and visible for a long distance.

The mist made him cough. After blundering along in it for about fifty metres he turned back, making for the last fence. Oddly enough, it gave him a small feeling of security. He walked along beside it, aware of smoke coming from the town. Two things then vied for his immediate attention. The first had to do with the town coming to life again, in spite of the curfew. The smoke was concentrated like a low dark mushroom growth over the area which he had just left. Flames were licking the edges of the spreading smoke cloud before it occurred to him that the ruin of the Zuidmaas

Hotel was on fire.

The second consideration had to do with his legs and the way in which his knees were being pumped higher at every step. Walking with his left hand on the top rail of the fence, he realised that he was walking uphill. There was a hill or a mound of some sort along the southern perimeter of the town between the polderland and the more permanent sandy soil.

In a land which was flat, the smallest hillock brought a kind of relief to the monotony of the landscape. He grinned briefly in the darkness, recollecting that a certain village football team in the north of France called themselves *Les Montagnards* (the Mountaineers) simply because they had a small hill within their boundaries.

This hillock he was climbing amounted to some 65 metres. It would make a good lookout point for a man who did not know his local geography, shortly after dawn. As he climbed, he studied the developing situation back there in the town. A fire engine of sorts was spraying the damaged shell of the old hotel. The locals were helping the military because it had been their building before belonging to the Germans, and they hoped it would be theirs again some time soon.

Britwell wondered what Christina would do when it was time to go to work that day. With an effort he recollected that this time was early Tuesday. The airborne armies of the allies would soon have been in action for forty-eight hours. A long time to be on the job at a stretch, with no helpful news from the south of the orthodox ground forces pushing northwards to relieve them. He brooded over Christina, hoping that she had kept her 'nose' clean during her evening run. He had no possible means of knowing that she had put her whole future in jeopardy by being involved in a head-on engagement between the Resistance and troops headed by men who were tracking her movements.

Nearing the top of the mound, Britwell tried to clear his thoughts. He remembered what she had said when they first made contact. In a way, his presence had made her frightened. He made her war effort too emotional. Maybe he ought to refrain from trying to link up with her again. She was a clever, resourceful girl, and she could take care of herself. Just so long as her reckless brother, Jan, didn't turn up and bring greater hazards with him.

If the hotel was destroyed as a communications base, the Abwehr might insist she went off somewhere else with them. Or, she might decide for herself to make a break, move to some other area where her misdemeanours were unknown. After all, she had relatives and contacts in two or three provinces of Holland. That much, Jan had made clear.

The summit levelled out abruptly. More slowly, the mist became thinner and wispy between the mound and the town, where the fire fighters were as busy as ever. He laid aside the Schmeisser and sat himself down, pulling up his knees and bracing his arms around them for warmth. Schulz's uniform was not a bad fit, but the German had been wider round the waist than the present occupant, and that meant the trousers and tunic were puckered under the belt. A man could get a bad stomach chill in a very short time in this sort of temperature. He pulled out the bayonet from the scabbard at his waist, and occupied himself by sharpening it on a stone.

Even as the steel rasped on stone, he wondered if he would ever use it in cold blood. Probably never. And how much longer was he going to masquerade as a German trooper, after daybreak?

Several small consecutive explosions buffeted the earth and blasted the smoke and flames skywards. The suddenness of it, and the knowledge that it was the hotel which had suffered again had a profound effect on Britwell. He rose slowly to his feet like a wraith, wondering about the unexpected eruption and how it had been caused.

Two or possibly three seconds elapsed as he stood there with his eyes screwed up and staring across the roof tops. He neither saw nor heard the other figure rise up from the ground just beyond him, but he soon became aware of it. The shape came at him like a wild beast. The face was blackened and the hands were gloved. A tight black cap topped the skull.

He just had time to turn through a few degrees to face the direction of the unexpected menace when a pair of heavy German binoculars swinging on a strap caught alongside his face. This time the right side suffered. He shifted his weight sideways, threw up his arm to protect himself further and was raked across the shins with the same article.

His antagonist got to the discarded bayonet before he did, and after that he knew he was fighting for his life. The other came at him with the bayonet held out in front, a two-handed attack backed by lethal determination.

In his borrowed clothing, Britwell was at a loss how to offset this deliberate personal attack. Should he simulate the German language, or should he cry out in brusque English that he was a fake? His brain was not reacting very well to his latest setback, but physically he was lucky. The extended blade — newly sharpened — was only a few inches from his chest when he made a grab at the wrists which held it.

In this he was lucky. He allowed himself to go over backwards, risking the shock of harsh contact with the earth. He then held onto the wrists with all his strength and swung the bayonet wielder over to one side.

In Dutch, meanwhile, his attacker muttered: '*Harry Britwell may have died in that demolished hotel, mijnheer, but you will not survive him for more than a minute or two!*'

Britwell identified his name without making any sense of it. The pair of them were still fighting hard when his assailant stuck the ground quite hard, still clinging to the bayonet. The dark beret flew off the head and the fine bell of auburn hair burst out into the open, brushing the pseudo German's face. He gasped.

'Christina? What the bloody hell is going on?'

The girl gasped even louder. As though by mutual consent, their powerful grips on the bayonet and wrists were relaxed.

'Christina, it's me, Harry. I had to borrow this rig-out to get away from the hotel! Relax, will you?'

'Harry, I can't believe it. I made sure when that ammunition blew up just now in the basement that you must have been killed! I came up here to check on your movements through the binoculars as soon as it was light. But, as I said, I had given up hope. I was in a killing mood, thinking you were dead. I — I might have killed you with my own hands! Just think of that! Horror of horrors! Hold me, Harry!'

Britwell hugged her in his arms, aware that she was shaking. The shock rather than the chill mist had upset her equilibrium. He rocked her against him and now for the first time he did not want the sky to brighten.

He said: 'What a long, nerve-wracking night it has been. And now, when dawn comes, we'll be in *more* trouble. But you can rest a while. I'll keep alert. If you're not too tired, tell me what — if anything — happened to you earlier in the night. I was wondering if you were in any way mixed up in the shootings somewhere west of town.'

'All right, Harry, I'll tell you about it. But then we'll have to move on. The two of us. This little town has suddenly become too hot for the pair of us. Earlier, I had thought to go back to work and try to bluff it out. But that was before the bomb hit and finding you here.

'Like I said earlier, my aim was to get some of the local Resistance boys to break you out of jail . . . '

10

Lunch was a hurried affair in the small hamlet of Oostmaas about two to three kilometres east of Zuidmaas. Shortly after dawn the runaway couple had widely skirted the scene of the night's adventures and proceeded eastward with nothing more than self-preservation motivating them at that time.

Erik Nottet, the nephew of Christina's landlady in the previous town, received them with some trepidation when he first saw Britwell's German uniform, but the situation was rapidly smoothed over as the Englishman explained who he was and how he came to be dressed as a German. In fact, Nottet spoke really fluent English, and he had from time to time read articles written by the war correspondent in smuggled newspapers. He was definitely pleased to meet a British war correspondent with sufficient initiative to break out of the Zuidmaas Hotel when it was fully manned and the Germans alerted for an attack by the Resistance.

Erik, who was a printer by trade, so far unwound as to show his two unexpected visitors his radio transmitter. He had his wife move around the village looking for a suitable change of clothing for Britwell who needed to be out of his German clothing without delay.

Oddly enough, the required gear, a chocolate coloured outfit more or less tailored along the lines of a British soldier's uniform came out of the dressing up box in the village school. The children surrendered it readily enough because no one in the school was big enough to wear it. The paratrooper's red beret was sent along with the teacher's compliments. She, a matronly spinster, would have liked to keep it but she was afraid that one day the Germans would find out she had it, and that in some way they would put pressure upon the school.

Erik's wife, Atje, bespectacled like her husband, turned out a few items of clothing for Christina, while Britwell changed into his new gear in the basement. The two runaways came together again and, for a time, wondered what their next plans ought to be. Although they were undecided, it was clear that they ought to get out of the small hamlet before their presence began to attract attention.

The local Resistance were very proud of the way Erik had kept up his contact with Resistance leaders based in London, but they were constantly on the alert and wary of anyone passing through: especially since the remarkable incidents in Zuidmaas the previous night.

'I am sorry to hasten your departure, Mijnheer Britwell, and yours Christina, seeing that my aunt has mentioned you so often. But it is best to move on. I have to admit that the arrival of our allies from the skies has made things difficult. In a month or two it will be easier. My wife and I wish you well,' Erik concluded sincerely.

They shook hands all round, and Atje embraced her visitors; and just before they were due to leave, Erik removed his horn-rimmed spectacles which had steamed up in the general excitement, and made a suggestion.

'Just before you leave the hamlet, make your way up the old church tower. If you use those binoculars, you might see something interesting to the north. But you'd have to hurry. Understood?'

Buoyed up by good wishes and countless little acts of generosity, the pair left their hosts, hurried down the lane which was flanked by the two shops, and made their way to the old church. The nave and aisles, in fact, the whole of the main structure had been demolished at an earlier date: but the tower still stood, and even that was minus its bell, as the Germans had removed it either to use its metal for war materials, or to prevent its being used as any sort of a signal.

The door in the tower looked as if it had never been opened in years, but it gave way with surprising readiness when Britwell put his shoulder to it and held it open for Christina to pass through. Three crude wooden floors above them, something hastily stirred.

Britwell felt over the Schmeisser

machine-pistol which he was now carrying along in a hessian sack. He exchanged glances with Christina, who was a little frightened but smiled weakly.

'I think it can only be a rat, Harry. Maybe the bayonet is all you need to protect us. In any case, let's hurry. I have this feeling we'll be too late if we don't.'

As they emerged into the top level, where the bell had originally been, the 'rat' challenged them. He was a small boy, Christiaan Koch, who every now and then disappeared on the way to school so that he could watch for signs of the war from the top of the tower.

Christina said: 'So, this is where you spend your time, is it? Your teacher will be interested to know where you hide instead of attending school.'

'Oh, but the lessons are boring when there are young men just a few years older than I am helping to push the Germans out.'

'Off with you, then, and mind you don't tell anyone who you saw up the tower, eh?'

Christiaan lifted his cap with the

broken peak, replaced it and faced his interrogators with a cheeky grin. He thought he had the means to barter a bit more time up the tower. Britwell, who did not have sufficient command of the Dutch language to argue with him, withdrew the business end of the Schmeisser from its sack and that had the desired effect. Christiaan did not stop running down the wooden stairs until he reached the bottom where they heard the door slam and saw him run off down the lane.

Britwell was chuckling to himself while Christina lined up the glasses on the north and brought them into focus. She showed excitement almost at once. During the morning, the weather had cleared up and visibility was reasonably good.

'I can already see what it was Erik hinted at, Harry. Here, you take the glasses. You'll understand more, I suppose.'

Pushing his sun glasses up onto his forehead, Britwell put the binoculars to his eyes and followed the line of

Christina's pointing finger. 'Ah, yes, another airborne armada is just going in!'

Christina leaned closer to him, resting on his shoulder. She felt his body stiffen as he reacted to what he saw. 'Harry, what is it?'

'There's far too much anti-aircraft activity for my liking! Our troops on the ground should have silenced the Germans in the area before this lot arrived over the dropping zone! I don't like it at all.'

The thunder of guns carried to them through the open sides of the bell platform underlining the terrifically hostile reception awaiting the tugs and gliders unhurriedly arriving over the D.Z. in and around the woodland west and north of Arnhem.

Britwell talked through his teeth. 'One glider has just crashed into a tree and caught fire.' He groaned. 'Another casualty. Glider hit in flight and breaking up. I can't stand to watch it!'

He surrendered the glasses to the girl and nervously polished his sun glasses. He said: 'Over to the east, all may be going well, but that northern sector, the Arnhem area, is having a really bad time. And they've got the longest time to wait for relief from the south. I wonder how far the 2nd Army has progressed out of Belgium since the operation began? After all, it's been over two days now!'

Christina tried to soothe him with gentle words, but she too was troubled by what she saw. After a pause, he asked: 'What's happening now?'

'Most of the gliders are down now, and intact. There *have* to be casualties, Harry. It's no use worrying your head about it. There, that's the last one down. Here come some planes now. And parachutes! They're dropping supplies by parachute. Take a look for yourself, my love.'

At first, as he studied the blossoming parachutes he seemed relieved, but soon his morose expression was back in place. She merely thought he was depressed, but he was noticing that many of the floating 'chutes appeared to be drifting in the direction of the flak batteries.

More trouble for the British Airborne Division.

Presently, Britwell made excuses to leave their vantage point. His companion knew that he was troubled by what he had seen. She did nothing to make him stay. Together, they made their way back to the river where they located a small wooden warehouse, a store for diesel oil used by bargees who were still permitted to ply the waterway with vegetables and dairy produce. As it was nearly 200 metres clear of the hamlet it was thought to be safe for them to rest up in. In spite of the cloying smell of diesel oil, the two of them dropped off to sleep within a few minutes of their arrival.

Around four in the afternoon, a long narrow diesel barge chugged up from the direction of Grave, and Petrus Broekman, a bearded, hook-nosed ageing Amster-dammer, came ashore with a few smuggled goods for the local people and stumbled upon the two sleepers in the shed.

He was startled enough to go for a pistol, but Christina roused herself and explained their presence. Britwell awoke two minutes later looking and feeling guilty. Christina introduced the two of them, and Britwell then assisted with the fuelling of the boat.

Broekman, a pipe smoker, offered to try and satisfy his curiosity when he asked for recent developments in the fighting.

'Mixed, my friend. Good things and bad things. I can tell you that the Americans have captured the road bridge over this river, the Maas, at Grave. And they also control the Maas-Waal Canal, which is further east.' Christina translated.

Hearing these things, Britwell relaxed a little and hugged Christina in both his arms. Broekman would have broken off then, seeing that he had pleased them, but Britwell perceived what his informer was about and demanded to know more.

'In the British sector, things are not going well. A small handful of British paratroops are doing their best to keep the main road bridge intact. Others are penned up in their dropping zone in the wooded country. Reinforcements have several times tried to get through to the bridge to strengthen the hand of those defending it. So far, they've met with little success. The main bridge still is intact, but the Germans have managed to put powerful Panzer units across it, and these are moving south to intercept the Americans and to tackle the bridge at Nijmegen.'

Britwell nodded as Christina interpreted further. His hands gripping her arms almost bruised her flesh without his knowing. Broekman repeated that his news was mixed, and said he wished it had been all good.

He added: 'I'm going down river now. If you're still about later this evening I'll be back again, going the other way. Or, you could take a ride with me.'

After due consideration, the couple refused the tempting offer of a ride, and said they hoped to see Broekman again. They helped him to cast off, and when he had gone, retired to their wooden hut to resume their rest. Britwell soon dropped off to sleep, but this time he twitched and writhed about and perspired.

The girl stripped off her track suit and then finally her other clothes. She dabbed his brow, unfastened his top clothes and gently pressed her body against his. In a little while, the tensions seemed to leave him. He felt and knew her presence and gently clasped her to him under the faded blanket which Broekman had left, oblivious to the permeating stench of diesel oil.

11

Every now and then when the screening blanket threatened to slip off their bodies, either Christina or Britwell rolled to one side and then the other, so that they had it tightly entwined around them once again.

At the end of a long kiss, Christina saw a far away look in her lover's eyes. 'What are you thinking, Harry? Please tell me.'

'I was thinking that I never really expected to find you when I came to Holland for that express purpose. Nor, as a bonus, did I expect to make love to you in an evil smelling old shed at five o'clock on a September afternoon.'

'Was that all?' she whispered.

'What else could there be? Bliss is a place of small dimension tucked away somewhere in a person's life. One stumbles on it often without warning. As I did. Yes, there is something else. You know how I admired your figure in a track suit, and in a swim suit? Well, I like it a whole lot more in the birthday suit, and that's a fact. Your other auburn trimming blends in with even more freckles, as if you make a habit of wearing the scantiest of clothing in sunny weather.'

Her body nudged him subtly as she laughed inwardly. 'Ah, but I am not as sunburnt as you are, Harry. I'm sure you weren't wearing a top coat all that time you were in Burma. And do you know, I can fit two fingers into the grooves left by your war wounds? You should have had medals for those.'

He smiled his most relaxed smile. 'A non-combatant does not expect medals. He is supposed to stay out of the combat.'

She shrugged against him. 'I like it when you open your eyes really wide and relax your expression to look at me.'

'Why is that?'

'Because then I can see the white crowsfeet wrinkles at the outer corner of your eyes in every detail. I haven't examined a man so closely since I was three years old — in my father's arms.

Please, make love to me again, slowly. Because bliss may disintegrate. We may lose it again. Harry?'

Britwell obliged. Fifteen minutes later, Christina was half asleep. He gently disengaged himself and helped her into a navy blue roll-necked jersey which Mevrouw Atje Nottet had discovered for him.

'Christina, you have slight shadows under your eyes. Sleep a little longer, and be relaxed. Me, I'm going to make some notes on that pad Erik found for me.'

The girl shrugged the soft hair at the nape of her neck out of the jersey. She opened her eyes very briefly to look at him. Next, she pouted her lips towards him. 'If you kiss me, I will.'

★   ★   ★

The time was a little after half past six when they put love and rest aside and tried to discuss their immediate future. The river had been placid, unused after Broekman's departure. Christina had a hankering to talk again with the women of the little hamlet. Her reason did not amount to anything much, except that she liked pleasant company of her own sex. A reason which she would not have admitted to herself had to do with whether Atje and the other women could tell how much she was in love with Harry.

Although he was very wary about their present plight, and the hazards they ran, he agreed to go back with her and to take along the few items of smuggled black market goods which Broekman had put aside for some of the locals. At ten minutes to seven, they had retraced their steps over the two hundred metres between the diesel shed and the hamlet, except that on this occasion they had used the narrow tow path.

Suddenly, what had begun as an idyllic stroll turned into the beginning of a nightmare. Three speeding German vehicles came up a winding road from the south and entered the hamlet by the lane which the lovers would have taken had they returned to Oostmaas the same way as they left.

Britwell pushed Christina down on the path between two allotments which stretched from the tow path, up a gentle slope, and came out behind the row of four terraced cottages where Erik Nottet lived. He went down on one knee beside her, and lowered to the ground the heavy tinned eatables which were in the sack with his machine-pistol.

The vehicles were a jeep, a mobile gun and a half-track troop carrier. The jeep was ahead. It rounded the square in front of the church tower, accelerated between the main row of terraced houses on the south side and the butcher's and the grocer's on the other.

Just beyond the shops, the driver turned the jeep to the right and brought it to a halt across the road with its bonnet facing towards Erik Nottet's small printing works which stood back a yard or two from the other buildings. The mobile gun stopped in front of the butcher's shop with its single menacing barrel pointed directly across the street at the houses, while the bulky troop carrier pulled up alongside the tower and disgorged no less than twenty troopers who formed up in a double crescent alongside of the vehicle with their rifles and automatic weapons at the ready, and their senior N.C.O. almost lifting off the ground in his impatience to go into action.

The C.O., a tall hook-nosed Colonel with a monocle, leisurely stepped out of the jeep, oozing authority and flicking one hand with a pair of gloves held in the other. He gave a quiet instruction to a captain who was accompanying him, and that resulted in a loud command being issued to the waiting troops and their N.C.O.

Six men left the rest of the squad and moved at speed towards the printer's establishment. Two went round the back, one more at each side, and the remaining pair entered the building. One or two children who had been playing in the street rapidly withdrew into their parents' house.

Shoppers at the butcher's, which was still open, moved further into the building and attempted to blend into the shadows. Watchers suddenly terrified watched cautiously from behind curtains and hoped that this display of force was only a bluff.

Almost at once, Erik Nottet with his spectacles pushed up on his lined forehead and a smear of printer's ink under his ample chin, was hustled out into the street followed by his aged assistant, the bald, stooping and bow-legged village character known as Old Vincent.

These two were ringed beside the jeep by other German personnel while the Colonel and the captain strolled into the printery accompanied by an N.C.O. and two troopers. Unlike the buildings on either hand, the printery was a single storey edifice. Soon, it became clear that an all-out search was being made there, presumably for some sort of literature forbidden by the Germans. There was a lot of noise, as if machinery was being banged about and desks and furniture being overturned. For extra measure, a trooper knocked the glass out of a rear window with the butt of his rifle. This act was calculated to affect the nerves of the villagers, and it certainly succeeded.

The Nottet cottage was the nearest of a series of four on a terrace a little to the

175

rear of the 'works' and alongside of it. Atje slipped out at the back door of her cottage and looked across the backs to the rear of the printery. Clearly, she was in a quandary and did not know what to do for the best. The oldest of her three children, a boy of seven, noticed Christina when the latter bounced to her feet about fifty yards away down the allotment and waved her hand.

The child informed the mother, who sent the child indoors and gestured for Christina and Britwell to stay where they were and keep out of sight. A trooper came round the side of the printery. The very sight of him was enough to send Atje scurrying back indoors.

The uproar in the low building went on perhaps for another five minutes. During that time, the small population tensed up still more, particularly the Nottet family. Down the allotment, the two observers were equally distressed.

'Harry, can you imagine what's going on? Erik is under some sort of suspicion. I can't help thinking someone has told them the Nottets have been helping us!'

Britwell, whose arm was across her partly as an embrace and partly as a safeguard to keep her out of sight, shook his head. 'I don't think so. My guess is they think Erik is publishing an underground newspaper, and that's very serious. I hope for the sake of the family they don't find anything incriminating. Incidentally, if they'd happened along five minutes later, they could have captured the pair of us without difficulty and had a first class excuse for reprisals. Now, keep quiet. I want to listen.'

The folks who lived on the street saw the searchers come out of the building empty-handed. Erik was pushed along roughly, prodded by rifle butts, until he was standing in front of the Colonel. A short, sharp question and answer session took place. First of all, denials about an underground newspaper ever having been printed in Oostmaas.

After that, Erik pointed out where he lived, and the search took another turn. Three troopers moved into the cottage and hustled the woman and her three children out into the street. Others turned the place over. Plant pots were knocked down and smashed. Pictures hooked off the walls. Chests in the bedrooms were overturned.

Again, the searchers failed to find anything. Those working the bedrooms came below again. One of the stoutest dragged Atje's sewing machine off the low wide window-ledge in the sitting room. The same trooper stuck his boot on the ledge and the way he did it was sufficient to show that the space under the ledge was hollow.

Almost at once, the secret hiding place for the transmitter was revealed. The N.C.O. called in triumph for the Colonel and the hearts of all the Dutch who heard it, sank. The Colonel inspected the sight after polishing his monocle on the table cloth. He gave a quiet order and at once the whole squad of troopers went into action.

In two or three minutes, every living person in the village with the exception of three babies and an old bedfast woman was hustled into the square or the area between the houses and shops. Apart from the very young ones among the fifteen children involved everyone knew what must have happened. In searching for evidence of a non-existent secret newspaper, the Germans had blundered upon the all-important radio transmitter.

Erik Nottet, Old Vincent and the beetle-browed butcher for extra measure, were dragged along to the church tower and lined up in front of it. Atje tried to break through to be with her husband, but she was held back by neighbours.

The Colonel spoke. 'So, Mijnheer Erik Nottet has been running a radio transmitter for the Resistance. He is a fool. He won't be given the chance to do the same sort of work for the Third Reich. That sort of alternative is not available any more. Instead, an example will be made of your printer and the two men standing near him.

'What a pity, you, Nottet, were not content to stay in your village and carry out your lawful work. In seeking to interfere in the conduct of the war, you are now to lose your life!'

Erik spread his hands, which was as near as he was able to go towards pleading. Several of the older villagers raised their voices in protest, but the sudden swing of automatic weapons in their direction reduced them to silence. The Colonel nodded to the captain who shouted: 'So die all traitors to the Reich!'

The captain's signal was relayed by the N.C.O., whereupon Erik Nottet, Old Vincent and Verkerk, the butcher, died under a withering hail of fire from three machine-pistols some twenty feet away. The stricken villagers started to move away, but they were warned to stay. The demonstration of German power was not yet over.

No one was allowed to disperse, or to go near the new corpses until the printing works had been destroyed by three cannon shells fired at point blank range. Two minutes after that, another shell blasted in the front of the Nottet cottage.

At the rear, Christina, who had been forcibly held down by Britwell while the shootings occurred, broke free from his grasp and ran up the back garden of the printer's house just as the shell was fired into the front of it. She was no more than fifteen yards away when the window over the transmitter erupted outwards, along with some of the stone work.

The surprise shocked her, brought her to a halt in a way which nothing else could have done. But for this shock, Britwell would not have been able to overhaul her. As it was, he was in time to drag her behind a box hedge and grip her with his hand over her mouth while the demolition experts prowled the rear to make sure that they had achieved their aim.

After that, the troops withdrew, leaving the shocked populace to recover and bury their dead.

Christina cried and hammered the chest of Britwell for a minute or more. 'You should have done something! Surely you could have let me go! I am Dutch! I feel for them! It is not the same for you, an Englishman!'

He allowed her to weep, and gently dabbed the superficial cut on her cheek made by flying glass. She brushed him aside and started for the street without him, but before she was out of sight she turned back again and waited for him, holding out her hand.

In spite of the sorrow and the suffering, they were received by the mourning community without any signs of resentment. Christina helped with the laying out of the bodies in the school house and Britwell helped with the digging of the graves in the cemetery beyond the church tower.

Towards dusk, kindly villagers hustled them off in the direction of the riverside to await the return of Petrus Broekman, the bargee, who had hinted at the possibility of their going up-river with him. As they strolled along, arms across each other's backs, Britwell was thinking about their next move. It would make a pleasant change to journey over water for a while, but where should they make for?

In other words, could Christina be persuaded to turn her back on the north, the area where her father, mother and possibly her grandmother were residing at this time of strife and anxiety? Would she abandon those who might possibly need her and travel south with a man who loved her towards the allied lines and comparative safety?

Britwell queried: 'Where do you think we should ask Mijnheer Broekman to take us, Christina?'

The girl shrugged. 'Oh, somewhere clear of this unhealthy area. Anywhere on the north bank of the river where we can strike out towards my folks and your countrymen. It's no problem, is it?'

She surprised a remote look in his eyes, but they cleared again to the steady greenish-blue which she knew so well. He was reluctant to answer in case he communicated his fears for their future. So, instead, he lowered his weapon sack, embraced her in the gathering gloom and kissed her fervently and with great gusto.

He hoped that she of *all* the Dutch, of *all* women, would survive the war.

12

Broekman, the bargee, chugged back into their lives in his sober fashion and took them on upriver. He listened sympathetically to news of the Oostmaas setback and tailored his comments in order to lift the burden of shock from Christina.

It pleased the girl to know that Broekman was probably related to her mother. A more startling revelation was that her brother, Big Jan, was back in Gelderland, skilfully helping the Dutch and hindering the enemy.

Britwell acknowledged Christina's joy over Jan, but he had secret misgivings about the reckless redhead and the trouble which followed in his wake. In a way, Jan's reappearance was working against the Englishman's cherished aim, for as long as the Dutchman was active further north there was no way of luring Christina towards the Allied lines and safety.

Further off, bitter fighting raged south of Nijmegen, constantly reminding them of the unrelenting struggle for the bridge corridor.

At dark, they went ashore on the north bank. Meeting with Broekman had been good for them. Britwell had shaved and composed his despatches for translation by Christina and transmission by the bargee. For two and a half hours, they slept in a fowler's hut. Christina was lethargic at one-thirty in the morning, but Britwell knew she was keen to reach the Waal river before dawn, and when she was fully alerted she moved over the unfamiliar rural territory with ease, seemingly guided by the rustle of reeds and bird cries near the tricky irrigation canals.

At last they detected the powerful flow of the Waal, which was the Rhine's main stream. They slowed down then, and became more vigilant, but no human hazards were detected and they swam across, towing their clothes on a piece of timber, until they found a shepherd's hut.

★ ★ ★

Christina made the breakfast in the shepherd's hut and a rather makeshift meal it turned out to be. While she was busy, Britwell moved out of the hut and milked a Friesian cow which appeared to have strayed far from its regular base. On his return, holding the milk in a serviceman's water bottle, he found a spread consisting of tulip soup, apples and a few biscuits which had a peculiar taste.

As they settled down to eat, Britwell had questions to ask: 'It isn't that I don't trust you, sweetheart, but I would like an idea of the menu. To me, it doesn't seem much like a Dutch peacetime affair.'

Christina wrinkled her freckled nose at him. 'We didn't ask you to come, Englishman. You must make the best of it. You have tulip soup, like most Nederlanders at this stage of the war.'

'What about the biscuits?'

'Bulbs go into the making of the biscuits, too, but you would have to ask someone else for the recipe. Perhaps, later today, we shall meet with other Dutch people and become more deeply involved.'

'Where are we on the map, now?' Britwell queried.

The girl took out a crumpled map given to her in Oostmaas. She spread it out, emptied her mouth of biscuit and pointed.

'About here. Between the Waal river, which is at our back, and this road west which forms a T-junction further east with the north-south linking road between Nijmegen and Arnhem.'

Britwell nodded and studied the surrounding details. 'Most of the heavy fighting seems to be in two distinct directions now.' He pointed them out, and the girl identified them as the Nijmegen area, south of east, and Arnhem and district to the north-east.'

Talk of deeper involvement after a period of relative calm seemed to trim their appetites. Christina made it clear that they had one more river to cross before they could claim to be in the area of the British dropping zones and the places where her brother, Jan, was said to have been active.

It was around eight o'clock that they moved away, wondering what fate had in store for them: whether they would survive, or if they had reached their judgement day. A stooping old shepherd with a complexion like cracked parchment accosted them as they were crossing territory used for grazing by his hundred head of lean sheep.

Christina's enthusiastic Dutch soon convinced him that they were genuinely in favour of Dutch liberation. He then took his stained clay pipe from between his lips and told them where to find two small, old battered bicycles which would help them on their way north.

By that time, September of 1944, Holland was full of bicycles. In fact, German personnel often used to ride the two wheelers along country lanes, riding on the rim because the tyre had given out and there were no replacements. In the dry ditch where they discovered the bikes under an old square of tarpaulin, the auburn-haired girl enthused.

'Real tyres, my love! But they don't

have much tread left on them so we'll have to go steady. Which do you choose?'

'The one with the crossbar, of course,' Britwell remarked bluntly.

Christina, who had already fancied that one, gave it over to him, but he found that the blocks of the front brake were tight against the rim and he had to cut a sliver away from the two blocks with the German bayonet before he could make any progress. The girl's model lacked paint, but ran freely: in fact, too freely, because the brakes scarcely functioned when squeezed on at full. Britwell did not approve of that kind of inefficiency, but he concluded that they would not be travelling very fast and that no serious accident was likely to occur.

The time was nearly ten a.m. when they paused at the top of a slight up-gradient for breath, and witnessed the arrival of yet another air armada from England. Still breathing hard, Britwell focussed the binoculars on the distant sight to the north, while Christina tried to identify the panoramic landmarks in between.

At first, the anti-aircraft fire was modest, but within two minutes every gun and flak battery in the vicinity of the low-flying planes was pumping shells into the sky with devastating results. Scores of gliders headed for what seemed to be a relatively small landing ground. Ahead of them, many-coloured parachutes were peppering the sky and drawing automatic fire.

Unbeknown to himself, Britwell was swearing. Christina queried his exact remarks and he put her off. 'I was thinking what it would be like if there were men dangling from those parachutes instead of canisters.'

Christina took over the glasses. She saw that many gliders were crashing and that lots of the canisters seemed to be falling beyond the hostile flak batteries. Britwell, however, was not listening. He had just come to the conclusion that the plight of the British would not be appreciably improved from the sky. Everything for them would depend upon a breakthrough from the south.

★　★　★

The British jeep started to come down the road from the east in low gear while Britwell and Christina were still taking in the view on the high ground. After blundering around in the lanes between the Waal and the Lower Rhine for several hours and being virtually cut off from British forces, the small outfit was heading westward away from trouble and with no clear idea of how to get back inside the British perimeter.

Secured across the bonnet was a door. Attached to the door and literally strapped down on it was the pained body of one Captain Peter Birks, a Reconnaissance Corps officer who had volunteered for the Arnhem business, and received a painful wound in his back for his trouble. Shrapnel had done the damage. He had a fairly large hole in his back, which was uppermost, had lost a lot of blood and the other men with him believed that his spine had been affected by the injury.

In the back of the jeep and with their condition doing anything but improving due to the uncertain jolting ride were two other wounded soldiers also in the traditional army khaki dress. Corporal Dickie March was a broad stocky paratrooper in his late twenties with a painful bullet hole through his right thigh. March, a regular soldier in peacetime, had a short upper lip which revealed his gapped teeth when he frowned and bulbous brown eyes. Those who travelled with him thought his wound had taken all the fight out of him, but basically he had a secret worry. When on leave he was a great womaniser, and he had fears about whether his sexual prowess would be affected by this uncalled for wound high up his right thigh.

Next to March at the back was a private paratrooper who looked like an advertisement for punch-drunkenness. Jack Profitt was four years younger than Corporal March, but his cauliflower left ear and the scar tissue on his eyebrows and chin made him look older. This character had a troublesome wound in his left arm, and to help keep it tight across his chest he had kept on his hip length jumping smock.

Sam Bexworth, another long-service

regular soldier, had taken over as driver for this impromptu sortie. He had so far escaped any sort of physical damage, but his temper had not improved as the wounded were picked up and brought along in the jeep, which had so far changed its status as to resemble an open-topped ambulance.

Finally, the man in charge, Lieutenant Ray Mingle, a glider pilot turned Reccy officer, was beginning to feel less and less confident as the minutes went by.

He was thinking: If we don't shake off that damned self-propelled gun before we go much further, they'll run us straight into the arms of some Panzer outfit, or another. Unless this sod of a jeep packs up on us, in which case we have to surrender to the troops following us.

He said aloud, 'Some bloody choice, for a man who's volunteered to do a reconnaissance!'

Bexworth at the wheel, the only man close enough to be in earshot, was not listening. 'Sir, I don't like the way this engine is labourin' an' what's more we're on the point of boilin' up any minute!

Just what we're going to do with that captain strapped across the bonnet when I 'ave to get at the engine, I don't rightly know! An' that's a fact!'

Lieutenant Mingle groaned and frowned. He was in the act of looking back in the direction they had come when the narrow lane converged with their route and the hurtling cyclist came down the hill with brakes squealing and totally ineffective. At once, the cursing sergeant slammed on the brakes and halted the jeep. The captain on the door was beyond loud noises, but the two in the back yelled out in pain, while Mingle threw up his Sten gun and abruptly turned in the direction indicated.

Christina van Vliet, who had been stiffened with terror for a time when the brakes failed to check her progress, now saw the vehicle in its stationary position ahead of her. She had just come to the conclusion that the door strapped to the bonnet would knock her clean off the cycle when Britwell yelled after her.

'Christina, for goodness' sake swerve! Pull out! Do you hear?'

She nodded, although her companion

was too far away to read the signal. Rather belatedly, she pulled in her limbs, stiffened against the shock of a premature crash, and managed to get her feet back on the pedals. With a last desperate effort, she cleared the bonnet of the jeep by swerving to the left, but her effort took her perilously close to the high bank on the other side of the road.

Another junction, wider and on the other side, caught her eye as she hurtled on. In trying to turn into it, her handlebar touched the steep bank and threw her out of balance. Off she came, her body flying through a graceful arc until she landed with a jarring bump on her shoulders and backward somersaulted.

Britwell came down the narrow lane a few seconds later, perceived the young lieutenant with his Sten pointing in the direction which Christina had gone, and promptly swung his bike — still travelling — across the road and in front of the target.

'Put your bloody gun up, man, she's one of ours!'

His voice sounded harsh, his throat

dry, but what he said and what the startled Britishers saw had the desired effect. Britwell leapt off his cycle and threw himself down beside the girl who was on all fours and rubbing herself ruefully. As she did the somersault, her dark beret had flown off her head revealing the magnificent bell of auburn hair which was one of her great womanly assets.

He said to her, as the other fit men approached: 'Damn it all, Chrissy, you might have broken your neck just now. It's bad enough trying to avoid the Krauts without doing wild things like that! I'm not sure you don't have a wild streak like your brother!'

Christina knew a sudden flash of anger at the mention of Jan, but something in Britwell's manner swung her emotions in another direction. 'Hell, Harry, you're beginning to sound like an old married man. Do you suppose these Englishmen will know we're having a lovers' tiff?'

Mingle and Bexworth, both frowning and perplexed due to previous troubles, grudgingly made themselves known, admitted that Britwell was probably who he said he was, and asked for help. Christina, as it happened, was only shaken and mildly bruised. A small khaki pack strapped to her back had broken her fall on first impact.

She surprised the British by opening up in English. 'What is it, lieutenant? It looks as if you had troubles before I hurtled into your midst?'

Mingle nodded. 'A blasted self-propelled gun has been pursuing us for the last couple of miles. We can't shake it off. On top of that, we have three wounded, one quite badly, and a jeep which is packing up on us.'

Bexworth added: 'The gears are not working at all smoothly. The engine's labourin' a bit, an' now the radiator's boilin' up. We'll 'ave to get the captain off the bonnet an' take a look-see.'

'We'll do all we can to help,' Britwell promised. 'That's why we were heading north.'

To move the door with its human burden took only about a minute, but even that seemed a long time when two shells of about 6 inch calibre came from some point out of sight to eastward and pitched in the meadow just north of the road.

The man with the prize-fighter's face spoke for the first time as the shells erupted and threw dirt into the road, and over a couple of browsing cows in the meadow.

'Hell's bells, lieutenant, you ain't goin' to leave us two sittin' 'ere in this open 'earse, are you, 'cause if you are, I'm getting out!'

Britwell exchanged glances with Christina. Without thinking it at all extraordinary he had read her thoughts. He put forward his idea, that of running the jeep into the cover afforded by the wider side road on the north side. Bexworth, whose nerves were in a state, just managed to check an outburst when on the point of opening up the bonnet.

Christina stayed by the man on the door stretcher while the sergeant drove the jeep the few yards necessary to afford it some shelter. Britwell did his bit by collecting the two bicycles and putting them out of sight up the wider entry. As he did so, a most remarkable thing struck him. All these men who had appeared out of nowhere with the jeep were bearded. And their eyes were ringed with dark marks which certainly meant lack of sleep.

Mingle had a fresh complexion which made his fine growth of fair beard and moustache unnoticeable until the observer was quite close. Sergeant Bexworth, on the other hand, had blue-black hair above and below his rather full red lips. Captain Birks' face lacked colour behind his short brown growth, and it did not show because he was strapped face downwards. The corporal with the thigh wound had a heavy brown facial growth, while Profitt, the bruiser, had the slightest facial growth of all. The hair under his helmet was short, brown and curly and hinted at some West Indian blood in his make-up.

Facial growth and black-ringed eyes. Certain pointers to the fact that the British were hard-pressed. Fighting night and day, no doubt, and probably a shortage of water to make life more complicated.

199

Bexworth cursed some more, but he managed to top up the radiator with extra water which Britwell had brought from the river. It was when he checked the oil in the sump that the sergeant really began to bemoan their fate.

Christina gave a small drink to the motionless man strapped to the door, while the others entered upon a bad-tempered, anxious council of war.

'That's it! I could pick out that wheezin' motor anywhere, any distance! I tell you they'll 'ave us, for sure!'

This was Dick March speaking. The sudden noise made by the self-propelled gun and the clatter made by its caterpillars as it negotiated a short gradient brought him out in perspiration. Had their own vehicle been in full working order, he would have kept calm: but with no conveyance, a man with a leg wound was on a hiding to nothing. Or so he thought.

Bexworth spat out. 'The oil level is far too low. No wonder the engine's not workin' properly. It'll seize up shortly. We need a miracle, or else our time is running out!'

Britwell, spurred on by the desperation in the men's voices, asked a lot of questions. Christina came back in time to hear him offering to create a diversion when the self-propelled gun arrived.

Grudgingly, Lieutenant Mingle approved the plan. 'All right, all right. So we'll take it you know how to use a Schmeisser. I'll slip you another couple of magazines. Will you use a grenade if we leave you one?'

Britwell nodded.

'One last question. To achieve the diversion you'll need a partner. Who are you going to have with you?'

The war correspondent looked very surprised. He raised his sun glasses and peered at Christina. 'Why, Miss van Vliet, here, will be all the help I'll need. She's been fighting longer than any of us, and she's a native of the district, so let's get things set up.'

*　*　*

The crew of the jeep went further up the lane, and stayed out of sight round the first bend. Christina was further down the road towards the west, beyond the two intersections. She had her bike with her, and her give-away bell of hair in full view. The weather was fine and the sheen on it magnificent. Britwell positioned himself on a small narrow knoll which overlooked the road at the first intersection. He had his Schmeisser beside him, and also a hand grenade, which Bexworth had told him was set to go off after four seconds.

As the labouring motorised gun with its clattering tracks came nearer and nearer, Britwell experienced a sudden thumping of the heart as the full force of what he had done, in placing Christina at risk, hit him. He wanted to shout warnings to her to take all sorts of precautions and to cut down on the risks, but it was too late.

The German vehicle was less than a hundred yards away. He risked a brief glimpse of it with the binoculars to his eyes and then hurriedly withdrew behind screening bushes. Two men with their heads sticking out of forward hatches: the driver and another, probably an observer.

Further back, standing on the platform to which the lean-muzzled gun was attached, were three men in German infantry uniform: a lieutenant and two other ranks. One of the privates was paying a lot of attention to a Spandau machine-gun fixed to the right side of the gun platform. Down the slope it came, its five personnel watchful, particularly the Spandau gunner and the forward observer.

Britwell breathed in as it went by beneath him. It was definitely in their 'area' now. The two side roads were just ahead of it, and Christina in her vulnerable position not many more yards further on.

No cries of surprise. Nothing to suggest a beautiful auburn-haired girl had wobbled into view on a veteran bicycle. The gun was passing the narrow lane down which Christina's brakes had failed when Britwell pulled the pin out of the grenade, licked his lips and nervously tossed it to his left, into the lane. At first it bounced on grass. His heart lurched as he thought it might do him more damage than them, and then it slipped from view, hitting the road surface at just about the duration of the setting.

The explosion sounded close and deadly. Underneath the war correspondent's flattened body the earth shook. His ears were still singing as the vehicle slowed and then speeded up, at an order from the officer in the peaked cap.

Britwell shifted his position then, as the observer took note of the girl in the brown suit wobbling on the bicycle and apparently startled out of balance by the sudden explosion. The Spandau operator, not an easy man to fool, turned his gun in the direction of the cycle, which was almost his undoing.

The grim-faced Englishman could only think of his sweetheart and her vulnerability. He wriggled forward several feet, put up the Schmeisser and fired a short burst in the general direction of the long-barrelled weapon and its attendant crew. His bullets, 9 mm. in calibre, ricochetted off the gun breech and sent the three men diving in all directions.

The driver accelerated again and the observer closed his hatch. In the rear, one infantryman had died instantly from a ricochet. The lieutenant and the other trooper were just straightening up and beginning to take notice of the girl again when they were cut down by the sudden scything fire from three weapons up the other side road.

The vehicle seemed to be going straight on, in spite of the setbacks, and Britwell was scrambling down to road level when another burst eliminated the driver who had never managed to get his head below hatch level. The caterpillar tracks slowly ceased revolving and the vehicle came gradually to a halt about ten yards past the intersection and the ambush.

The observer's nerves must have played him up exceedingly before Britwell rapped on the closed hatch with the Schmeisser barrel and urgently required him to step out. Sergeant Bexworth was just trotting up with a lethal expression on his face when the sole survivor rose into view and studied the face of the man in the sun spectacles kneeling behind him.

'You should have given 'im a burst, Britwell. We 'aven't time for prisoners in this man's war.'

'I thought we might damage the vehicle, sergeant. After all, ours is no good. We have quite a distance to go, I suppose, to reach the British positions.'

Hearing this sort of advice, Bexworth backed off. Britwell mimed for his prisoner to get out. Lieutenant Mingle checked the short, heavy-jowled observer for weapons and then seemed baffled. Britwell then assumed the initiative. Christina brought up the cycle with the inefficient brakes. She told the German to mount up and keep going, down the road.

He did so, glancing back once to know if he was going to be shot down from behind. Britwell, of all people, fired a short burst over his head and then the British party unwound sufficiently to think of the immediate furture.

13

By the time the British jeep had been booby-trapped and abandoned Britwell and Christina felt thoroughly involved on the side of the British. They felt the same concern for the deteriorating condition of Captain Birks, the officer with the back injury. He was clearly in pain although he had been given a liberal dose of drugs to dope him.

Christina estimated that they were five miles from Driel on the south side of the Lower Rhine. That meant that help could not be obtained for the wounded until Driel was reached. Corporal March and Jack Profitt were obviously in a much better condition than the captain but they, too, needed the urgent attention of a doctor used to surgery.

At first, it was deemed important to put a goodly distance between the scene of the recent clash and the small British party.

'We take the SP gun as alternative transport then, sir?' Bexworth queried.

Lieutenant Mingle thought this was a good decision, and he at once agreed, but no sooner had the captain on his improvised stretcher been put aboard the clanking tank-like machine of war with its clattering tracks than he realised that he had done a bad thing. Up the lane they went towards the north. Everyone on board, but all the wounded suffering, particularly the officer.

'We're going to have to use our legs very shortly,' Britwell opined, shouting in the lieutenant's ear.

Bexworth was doing the driving and although he did not find the work a very comfortable chore, the suffering of the wounded had escaped him. At the top of a short up-grade when the vibrations had seemed worse than before, Mingle called for a short halt. It was during this brief respite principly for the convenience of the wounded that another hazard was noticed. Across a valley towards the south-east, Private Profitt, putting the binoculars to his eyes with his good arm, made a discovery.

' 'Ere, sir, you remember that Jerry 'alf-track we thought was followin' along with this gun? Well, I just seen it again! They're still onto us. I don't figure this SP will be able to keep ahead of 'em at the speed we can safely do!'

Mingle took the glasses. He was in time to confirm the sighting of the troop transport before it dipped down, out of sight, on its way to the scene of the recent clash. Britwell and Christina, arm in arm for a brief moment and leaning against the nearest hedge, exchanged glances of alarm.

'Can we get to this hamlet, Driel, across country, Chrissy?'

'Of course. It'll be difficult with a man on a door and another on that bike. But we'll manage. I suppose they'll want to fire a few hostile shots, though, before they get round to abandoning the SP? Why don't you go and chat with the lieutenant? He listens to you.'

'I'd rather stay and make eyes at you, sweetheart.'

Reluctantly, Britwell moved off. He

kept glancing back because Christina had combed out her hair and fixed it again with her orange ribbon in a pony tail. After a hasty consultation, all personnel, and everything of value was taken off the gun.

Mingle called: 'Hurry up, Bexworth. Get her turned round. I want to fire what shells we've got over that hill to where we left the jeep!'

There was a lot of speculation as to the best way in which to train the German gun but, in effect, the muted sound of the booby trap going off helped a little with the firing. Mingle saw to the training and laying. Bexworth actually did the loading and firing, and Britwell assisted as the loading number.

None of them could see their target which was the formidable half-track containing over a score of German infantrymen, but after three rounds had been fired, a second explosion occurred which encouraged them to think that the petrol tank or some ammunition had gone up.

After firing the remaining three shells,

the party streamed down the slope. Bexworth and Britwell supported the stretcher. March rode gingerly down the hill on the other bicycle with his injured leg sticking out stiffly. Christina walked down, seemingly as light on her feet as ever, carrying weapons and making sure that the bulky Profitt did not come to any harm.

Mingle stayed behind long enough to soak parts of the vehicle in combustible stuff, and then he came after them with a burning improvised torch smoking in his hand. The whole party slowed to watch him hurl it back, which he did with great skill. There was just time to get round a bend and up a short slope onto meadowland before the first of a series of explosions went to work on the enemy machine.

Across rough open country, the going was slow. No more riding on the bicycle for a man with a leg wound. His partner could manage a few yards every now and then when the going was easy: otherwise the cycle was used for transporting arms. Bearing the heavy stretcher was particularly heavy going and the taking of the weight devolved upon the three fit men, Mingle, Bexworth and Britwell.

Christina was denied the right to take a hand with such heavy work, but she more than made up for her frustration in the matter by taking a lot of the weight of the thigh casualty as he hopped along between her and Profitt.

Necessary halts became more frequent. Tiredness cut out a lot of conversation and the actual responsibility for keeping away from the roads and possible hazards of location fell entirely upon the girl. Even she was beginning to show signs of weariness and strain by the time they moved through the allotments on the south side of a remote hamlet to the west of the village of Driel.

Three hours had elapsed since they abandoned the SP gun. Distantly to eastward, a cracked bell on some old church tower which had survived this far rang twice. Two o'clock on an afternoon when the sun was high after early rain. A nice bracing atmosphere for a battle to the death.

At the approaches to the hamlet, the

girl called for a halt.

The others moved around her, showing her the respect she deserved and awaiting her advice about mingling with the locals.

'My friends, you will be welcome here. But remember, you are very close now to the fighting. These villages along the south side of the Lower Rhine are likely to be visited at any time by the Bosche. So, as I am known at the hospital, here, give me a few minutes ahead of you. I'll take the bicycle. All right?'

The rest of the party were resigned to waiting. The fading captain was lowered to the ground on his bed. The rest spread out on a wide patch of grass which fronted the local cemetery and merely watched the shapely girl withdraw. Mingle and his party were puzzled about the relationship between the lean sun-bronzed war correspondent and the auburn-haired Dutch girl, but the former offered no sort of information and instead, he passed the time by asking about conditions within the British perimeter and the state of the bridge.

Things were much worse than he had

anticipated. He heard that two lesser bridges, one a pontoon erection and the other a railway bridge had long since fallen. As for the mighty arch of the road bridge, that remarkable construction had been held for about seventy-two hours by a mere fraction of the whole British force, amounting to just a few hundred. In fact, the estimated fit troops still holding on in the houses and buildings at the northern end of the bridge at the time when Mingle's small unit went astray was no more than two hundred.

All attempts to relieve the stubborn survivors of the 2nd Parachute Battalion and their meagre supporting troops had failed. Sooner or later, due to mounting pressure through German armour and artillery fire, coupled with the lack of food, dwindling supplies of ammunition and mounting casualties, the defenders would have to give in. Men could not fight on pep pills and sheer guts indefinitely.

'How about supplies and reinforcements?' Britwell felt forced to ask.

'Senior officers on the spot say that all

the proposed drop zones and supply zones are outside the territory at present held by our forces. That wouldn't matter, except that radio communication with those who count on the outside isn't up to scratch. Quite a number of the sets brought along for basic communications don't seem to have the range for the job. Things are looking bad for our boys, Britwell. You'll need to confirm what I've said and probably get permission to relay it — if you can find a set. But try not to make it sound *too* pessimistic. There are still useful fighting troops to come. The Poles! They're overdue, I believe. Held up at the other end, either by weather or transports. Hello, here comes an ambulance. Everything laid on, eh?'

A tired-looking young Dutch doctor with a middle-aged face stepped out of the rear of the ambulance flapping his white coat. He spoke kindly to the weary soldiers, arranged for Captain Birks' door stretcher to be loaded into the vehicle and for the other two wounded to take a ride. Apparently, the enemy were not in attendance at that time, although they were expected.

Britwell, Mingle and Bexworth sauntered along after the ambulance and came upon the hospital, a three storey building, if the basement was counted in. Every house in the hamlet, which was known as Broek, had an orange flag or a banner of some sort. Faces appeared in the windows, smiled and withdrew. They knew the battle for Arnhem hung in the balance.

Shells and bomb splinters often flew into the small settlement and made life unhealthy. Most of the aged and the very young had spent many hours in the cellars, the only safe place for anyone who had to be specially protected.

Christina met the weary trio at the door of the hospital. She had taken off her track suit, washed and changed into an off-white overall with a red cross on it. Her hair was tied back and topped with a white starched cap. She had worked in this self-same hospital before the German authorities grew suspicious of her spare-time activities and had her moved further south for interrogation and possible imprisonment.

She it was who conducted the soldiers and her lover into the basement, where they were given washing facilities and treatment for any wounds however small. They were then given food, although it consisted mainly of cabbage, soup and a few biscuits.

In the basement were the washrooms, the kitchens and the operating theatres. On the first floor were most of the beds. Others were located on the top floor in rooms rather than the small wards below. Christina rapidly became absorbed in the work of the medical team, and Britwell found himself holding on to Mingle and Bexworth before they left the hamlet to rejoin the British within their shrinking perimeter.

'You comin' with us, then, Britwell, to see what it's really like?' Sergeant Bexworth wanted to know. He would have liked to add some cutting comment about taking it easy instead with a nice Dutch 'bint' but he did not voice such a thought.

'Not right away, sarge. I've got some writing to do, and some observing, as well. I'll be in touch again, don't you worry. Right now, I'm going up on the flat top of that church tower to do some observing. I've enjoyed meeting you two, and I'd like to wish you luck. So long.'

They shook hands. Three clean, fit young men, two with distinctive beards and the other with some promising stubble. Britwell hurriedly climbed the tower of the local church so that he could see the British pair striding up the road towards Driel.

Fifteen minutes after he had started his self-imposed chores and become used to the brutal crash and thunder of shells, bombs and bullets, a rogue projectile from across the river burst on the corner of the tower parapet, resulting in his being concussed and rendered unconscious.

14

The rogue shell which shattered the corner of the church tower and put Harry Britwell in hospital with concussion and bruises was only a minor incident in the lives of the overworked hospital staff. They toiled only for the injured and they knew that from time to time their working conditions were likely to deteriorate.

However, although they had little time to call their own they at least could claim to be kept well up to date with any strategic developments. This was because the main telephone exchange in beleaguered Arnhem was manned entirely by Dutchmen, most of whom were entirely in sympathy with the efforts of the allied sky raiders, and some of whom figured in the Resistance. Messages between one German unit and another were deliberately delayed or even interfered with so that orders might possibly be misconstrued. Anything of interest to the

Resistance came out quickly and was relayed by many and various means to the local inhabitants and to senior officers of the airborne division wherever possible.

Thus, it was known in the latter half of Wednesday, September 20th, that the bridge over the Waal at Nijmegen had been taken due to superlative fighting by American General Gavin's 82nd United States Airborne Division and the British Guards Armoured Division which was a unit of the ground forces working its way up the corridor.

The front runners of the allied XXX Corps had orders to push on from Nijmegen to Arnhem at first light of dawn on Thursday morning.

This would have been great news for all, had the contingent which had been holding the fine road bridge against all comers for so long in Arnhem been more numerous, better fed, well stocked with ammunition and reasonably well rested. Unfortunately, they were tired almost to death, reduced to about one hundred and fifty in number, more or less pulverised through a continuous bombardment of bombs, shells, automatic fire, phosphorus shells and the like: starved and wracked by a growing and persistent thirst, and, possibly worst of all, reduced almost to impotence due to a chronic lack of ammunition.

As it was, the heroic fighters who had occupied the houses, schools and other buildings adjacent to the ramp on the north side of the bridge finally crumbled before an all-out onslaught by Panser grenadiers, who captured the British positions, one by one, hurling stick bombs into the ruins, and literally having to fight for every dusty smoking heap. This happened at about the same time as the allied tanks started to roll north from Nijmegen to Arnhem, the furthest outpost north on the preconceived corridor. Thursday: forenoon.

The last weary radio operator on the bridge perimeter announced the end, finishing his message with 'God Save the King.'

This tragic British setback at the Arnhem road bridge was also quickly relayed by the Dutch to sympathisers all around the area. It reached the two tired Dutch surgeons in Broek hospital about the time when they were starting their morning rounds of the patients. Uppermost in their minds was whether the surviving British airborne force north of the river, surrounded by the enemy and being continually squeezed around the perimeter, could survive long enough to be relieved by the spearhead tanks of the land army coming up the corridor from Nijmegen.

Time, as everyone knew, was the vital factor, since the brash assault from the skies had turned into a desperate operation for survival. Shortly before the surviving British forces were aware that the Arnhem bridge had fallen to the enemy, a vital link by radio was established between General Urquhart's headquarters in the shrinking British zone north of the Lower Rhine and the 64th Medium Regiment of artillery with the advanced units of XXX Corps in the region of Nijmegen.

Consequently, the hopes of those three thousand men still holding on under heavy pressure were raised when light shells began to hit the German forward units within a hundred yards of the British trenches and other defensive positions.

★   ★   ★

Christina van Vliet's emotions were in a flutter. In fact, they had been ever since Harry Britwell had been found unconscious on top of the church tower, the casualty of a shell which had never been aimed specifically at any target in Broek.

The girl had worked around the wards, two hours on and two hours off, all through the night of Wednesday and early Thursday. Frequently, she stopped in front of the bed on the middle floor where Britwell was sleeping. He was not badly hurt. Very tiny fragments of shrapnel had lightly scarred his back, while flying lumps of stone had knocked him out and given him mild concussion. He had been given morphine to kill his pain, and the time it was given and the amount of the dose was written on his forehead in indelible pencil.

In repose, his lean face had dignity. The white crowsfeet wrinkles showed starkly against his Burma sunburn at the outer ends of his eyes. With his head sideways on the pillow, his strong nose revealed itself to be more aquiline than Roman. The thin 'cat's whisker' lines of scar tissue, a hangover from another injury (with the Royal Navy) sustained earlier in the war, seemed to give his strong jaw line greater depth.

In her weaker moments, the Dutch girl wondered if she had enticed this man she loved unnecessarily far north. Had her eagerness to get into the Betuwe put his life in jeopardy? Had she acted in foolhardy fashion when she used her brother, Jan, as a personal excuse to hurry north to the Lower Rhine and the land of her relations?

After breakfast, she did a few exercises and stretched her legs in the narrow garden facing towards the river. Some time after that, a build up of chores took her to the basement where she alternated her time between the kitchens and the theatres until mid-morning.

The brutal cacophony of sound north of the river was in full swing, as tanks, SP guns, machine-guns, light and heavy, and artillery sought to subdue the British invaders before the ground troops from the south burst through to reinforce. There was noise in plenty, but nothing seemed to penetrate Britwell's assisted sleep.

About ten in the morning, the war correspondent started to stir. His brow was beaded with perspiration. His brain was working. Unconsciously, he murmured his thoughts aloud.

' . . . *as a reporting operation, sir, this Market Garden venture is something of a failure. The essence of it is water crossings. Two canals and three rivers. This far, I can honestly say I haven't set eyes on a single bridge. Oh, I know the road bridge at Arnhem is of the type known as arch suspension, but that's only because of good research, not reporting . . .* '

At this stage, he started to cough and this had the effect of bringing him nearer to consciousness. Almost like magic, Christina appeared beside his bed. She had tended many others in the hours since they arrived in the hospital. This time, however, she knelt beside the patient, held the cup to his lips and dabbed off his forehead with a cloth.

'Harry, can you hear me, love? This is Christina. Try and wake up, if you can. We have trouble. There's a small column of German troops in the hamlet. You recollect we're in Broek. You're in hospital with mild concussion and minor flesh wounds on your back.'

She paused, having spoken when his eyelids flickered. Suddenly his neutral-coloured eyes opened wide. He stared at her, smiled briefly and came alert.

'I recollect. It happened on the church tower. An unexpected shell. What time is it Chrissy? What day?'

'Just after ten o'clock. Your accident was yesterday. It's Thursday now. I think these Germans will come in here looking for British soldiers. I wanted you to know. How fit are you?'

He felt the padded bandages on his

back and experimentally moved his head in all directions. 'Hungry, thirsty. Back a bit sore. Head feels kind of rarified. Not too bad on the whole. Good treatment here, I guess. What will you do, if I pull out?'

Unexpectedly, tears formed a mirror over the intense blue eyes. He pushed back the bed clothes, removed his legs to the floor, glanced briefly at the patched pyjamas he was in, and then stood up, rather groggily at first. He then reached for the girl, embraced her and kissed her. Much against her feelings, she disengaged herself.

'Please, Harry, we've got to come to a decision.'

He released her, glanced around at the other seven or eight male patients and wondered what he should do. Was there, he wondered, any sort of temporary future in this building? The man in the bed nearest the windows in the south wall called a quiet warning. He could see the German forces spreading out and apparently making ready to vacate their transport.

'Get me a white jacket, Chrissy, and a stethoscope. I don't feel like nipping out yet. You can fix it with the doctors, can't you?'

For several seconds, the girl hesitated. It was the clattering of the tracks of a vehicle outside and the sharp words of command in German which spurred her to make an effort. She found a white coat hanging on a peg outside the ward. There was a stethoscope in the pocket.

She was licking her lips and looking anxious again when an opening pane of glass in one of the windows on the north side vibrated under the stress of a sudden blow. Choking back a cry of alarm, she crossed to the window, hastily undid the fastening and stepped back. Her surprise was phenomenal when a big red head which she had known all her life edged its way through the gap followed by the powerful shoulders and frame of her brother, Jan.

'Jan! This is hardly the time, or the place for a reunion. What the hell do you think you're doing, forcing your way in just as the Bosches arrive?'

'How are you, Chrissy? Nice to see you again! Now, don't panic. I need to pass muster as a patient for a while. You go about your duties. Make sure your doctors know they've got an extra man up here. That's all. We can't have them throwing a fit when the square heads come looking!'

Perhaps two Dutchmen of the bed occupiers were awake and alert to what was going on. The two British soldiers, Dick March and Jack Profitt, were both unconscious, having been liberally doped at the time when they were operated on to fix their wounds.

Jan van Vliet set about the business of concealing himself with all the elan of his earlier years in the Resistance when he had won for himself the reputation of a twentieth century Scarlet Pimpernel for his dash and daring. He had opened two cupboards normally left to the doctors when he noticed Britwell further down the ward shrugging into the white coat and adjusting it to fit his shoulders.

Jan frowned. Christina, very much on edge, had backed away from him to the door. The girl made gestures to her brother to keep his voice down, but the big Dutchman was so surprised at seeing another familiar face that he refused altogether to comply.

'Well, well, well! Doctor Britwell, I presume,' he remarked in English. 'You're just the man I need for an ally. I'll take this bed near the back window. Just take your cue from me, Harry, the master race won't be long!'

Pale behind her freckles, Christina slipped out of the ward, intent upon warning the doctors who were down below. In the meantime, Jan van Vliet produced a relic out of a cupboard. It was a pre-wrapped plaster cast, repleat with bandages. Britwell could have sworn that Christina knew nothing of such an object which could only have been prepared for the express purpose of deceiving the enemy.

Van Vliet worked the cast up his leg, called for and received help to haul up his limb with the traction pulleys attached to the ceiling. Britwell was hastily draping a white cotton bandage around the give-away red hair when he noticed the 'tools' which Jan had brought in with him. A bayonet and two grenades. Also a few magazines suitable for a Schmeisser automatic pistol.

In a flash, the Englishman realised that his unexpected 'ally' was intending to actually take on the Germans if and when they entered the hospital. The sack which Britwell himself had carried with him for many kilometres was now located under Jan's bed.

There was no time to protest. Outside, a curt order in the tone adopted by the arrogant youthful officers who had grown up entirely in the era of the Third Reich. The Dutchman nearest to the window murmured a further warning, eagerly picked by van Vliet.

'It is a troop carrier, the vehicle which has stopped outside. Other vehicles have moved on somewhere. An officer, one or two N.C.O.s and perhaps a dozen men. The officer and an awkward looking stooping fellow with a corporal's markings are coming quickly this way.

'A trooper is manning a Spandau fixed to the front of the vehicle. Another

N.C.O. follows the other two. Troops dismounting and spreading out. As if they are suspicious of trouble.'

Another barked command, right under the window, had the effect of silencing the Dutchman's commentary. Two men crossed themselves as the boots of the Germans rang on the corridor down below. Jan gestured for Britwell to examine the man nearest the south window, the one who had been commentating. Reluctantly, and with a strong sense of foreboding, the war correspondent complied. He had a feeling he was about to be pushed into doing something outside his normal code of ethics. And he was right.

Up the stairs came the officer and the tall corporal. The door was forced open in the customary fashion with the sole of a boot. In the two came, springing into a wartime gunman's crouch and facing in opposite directions. Britwell, who was pretending to examine the Dutchman nearest the south wall, looked up calmly nodded and shifted the stethoscope about a centimetre on the patient's chest. Near the other end, someone groaned.

As no one was paying any particular attention to the intruders, they gradually relaxed and adopted other tactics. In Dutch, the officer, a stocky barrel-chested fellow in his late twenties, with a peaked cap remarked loudly: 'Now listen to this, you Nederlanders, we are looking for men who should not be here. You understand?'

One of the Dutchmen nodded somnolently.

The kapitan sniffed, raised his black beetle brows and panned his Schmeisser. In English. 'Any Englishmen here, eh? Englanders?' His nostrils flared as his cunning eyes roved over the bed patients trying to detect a note of alarm somewhere. No response.

He then spoke in German, asking for any German nationals. This time there was a response. Jan, who was pretending to be badly hurt, groaned, turned his head on the pillow and answered. Britwell, whose heart was thumping hard with anticipation, listened carefully.

'Ja, ja. Wie viel uhr ist es?'

Jan sat up with an apparent effort,

glared in the general direction of the wall clock and subsided with an elaborate groan. Britwell felt like a similar utterance, but kept quiet. The captain moved nearer to him while the N.C.O. went cautiously over to the figure of Jan and began to bend over him. The atmosphere in the ward went suddenly tense. The captain had no idea what was in store for him but he backed against the partially opened window and watched very closely.

His attention was mildly distracted to what was going on in the open air when van Vliet made his move. The corporal bent to get something from under the bed. Jan promptly seized him, hauled him head and shoulders first across the bed and drove his bayonet all too thoroughly under the rib cage and through the heart. The corporal was pushed back while the scheming Dutchman slipped his leg out of the plaster and turned to face the captain with the Schmeisser in one hand.

Before the officer could react, Jan tossed the two grenades with a low sharp warning in English. Britwell caught and pocketed the two 'pineapples' and crouched ready for the next move. The German had only to move a few centimetres to menace them with his weapon. He could also summon help with a brief yell near the window, but something in the gaze of the remarkable Dutchman froze him where he was.

Britwell pushed the German's gun muzzle towards the floor and kept it pointing that way. Jan called for him to release the weapon which he did, although when he crouched back, recovering from his shock, Britwell figured he still had sufficient spirit to turn the tables on them.

Full of confidence, Jan said: 'You, Kraut, will open the window very cautiously, lean out a little way and call your men off. Back into the truck. Understand? Any mistakes an' you die without your Iron Cross!'

Before the instructions were carried out, there was a moment of extreme unease. And then the German turned, pushed the window further open and leaned out. Britwell was right behind him with the second Schmeisser lightly touching his back. Down below, the senior

N.C.O. called up to him.

'We're wasting time,' the Captain called back harshly. 'Call the men out of the building. Everybody back into the wagon. You hear? *Schnell! Schnell*!'

Britwell glanced over his shoulder. The Englishman was surprised to hear words in his own language from so close. 'You are English. I should have smelled you out before. You have the upper hand for a moment but it won't last, Englander! Mark my words!'

Down below, the men were moving out of the building and slowly crossing the open ground in the direction of the troop carrier. The man on the Spandau had his helmet off scratching his shaved head. Britwell felt himself on edge, and suddenly angered by this stocky German captain. All the time he was hesitating, the German was staring into his eyes, wondering if he had the courage to use the acquired weapon.

Van Vliet, still having the initiative, spoke to Britwell from the doorway. 'Deal with that damned officer right away! Then aim your grenades at the troopers down below. Make sure you get the man on the Spandau with the first. I'll be depending on you, my friend!'

With that, Jan ducked out, and straddled the balustrade, sliding down it like a schoolboy: still Britwell hesitated. The Dutchman fired a short burst into two or three troopers who had been slow to clear the entrance. The sudden burst of automatic fire alerted the whole platoon of soldiers out of doors. Britwell cursed. He tossed aside the Scmeisser, chopped the captain on the side of the neck and almost in the same motion reached into his pocket for the hand grenades.

The captain, who had been certain that Britwell would not react as the Dutchman had expected, was taken completely by surprise. The back-handed chop sent him staggering into the window again, where he over-balanced on the sill and fell head first to the hard ground below.

The man on the Spandau pointed up at the window, while the other troopers who had not yet mounted the vehicle turned around and started to bring up their weapons. Angry with himself for having been conned into this drastic lethal action, Britwell nevertheless did what was expected of him.

He bit out one pin, held the first grenade on one side and then bit out the other. It was as if his real self stood beside him as he went through this foolhardy routine. Fortunately, the second pin came out just as easily. He tossed the first grenade and had the satisfaction of seeing it drop in the vehicle behind the machine-gunner, while the second one overshot the mark and dropped on the far side of the vehicle where some of the troopers had taken cover.

About one second separated the explosions. The Spandau gunner and two men near him rose in the air, followed by the gun, which leapt off its mounting. While the immediate vicinity was too bright to see through and smoke and the more acrid smell of explosives were permeating everywhere, the second grenade erupted. This time, the whole vehicle lifted on the far side. Four or five men were killed outright and others staggered as the blast of the explosions spread. The big

Dutchman hurtled into the open where he fired the borrowed Schmeisser in a short deadly panning arc. Up above, Britwell also fired a short burst, picking off a man crouched in front of the wrecked carrier, who had somehow escaped death.

As the last apparent hazard was removed, Jan turned and looked up, beaming at his impromptu ally. 'Great going, Harry! You did a great job. And I always thought you were a man of peace!'

'I don't think the doctors or Christina will be so enthusiastic about what you've made us do here, Jan, but I'll come down now and help you to check the Germans over.'

Britwell was as good as his word. Oddly enough, every German with the single exception of the captain was dead. Christina had dashed out shortly after the Englishman and, to cover her relief, she crouched over the German and gave him a cursory check-up.

Britwell moved back to the girl, while her brother casually stuffed a couple of packets of German cigarettes in his pockets and lit one with a confiscated lighter.

'Chrissy, I'm sorry about all this. It all happened so quickly. I had to follow through, otherwise Jan might have been cut to pieces.'

'I understand, Harry. I'm glad you both survived, but it goes without saying we'll have to move on now. Doctor Geijssen, the senior surgeon, is furious about all the shooting. He'd have been out to say so before now, except that he's making one last big effort to save the life of Captain Birks, the door casualty.'

Ard Kaiser, the younger doctor with the tired expression, came out then. He was shaking his head at the two victors as he knelt down to make his assessment of the captain's condition. Britwell found himself waiting for the verdict like a man facing a potential murder charge. His confrontation with the officer seemed far more significant than the throwing of the grenades and the firing of the Schmeisser.

Kaiser, sensing his anxiety, looked up. 'This one was lucky. Bruises, contusions, maybe an odd chipped bone. Possibly concussed. He'll pull through. But your main concern is to get out as quickly as you can.'

He pointed to the scattering of male natives who were coming out into the open, knowing that something would have to be done to clear up the scene of the action before other German units arrived. He stood up.

'The local people will wheel the vehicle out of the hamlet and set it off down hill. Anything to get it out of our way. You and your ally, van Vliet, must dispose of the German dead with all haste. And then away! Christina won't stay behind without you. I think she's crazy, but she's coming with you!'

He called over his shoulder for the elderly orderly to bring a trolley, but Big Jan was ahead of him. Disregarding the unconscious officer's condition, he picked him up rather roughly and carried him indoors like a sack of potatoes. Still shaking his head sadly, the young-old doctor went back to his work.

Two frightened Dutch villagers came up with a hand cart. Britwell received it from them with a small show of dignity. It was intended to hold the bodies of the German dead on their way to the river. As soon as these two added their weight to that of the others who were pushing the troop carrier, it started to move and gathered momentum. Christina had gone indoors to collect all their gear and Britwell had managed to heave two of the dead onto the hand cart when Jan came out again.

'Go and collect your kit, Harry,' he suggested calmly, 'I'll manage.'

Britwell hesitated. He ran indoors, intent upon getting back into his brown pseudo-army suit. On the middle floor, he had a few minutes in which to say farewell to Dick March and Jack Profitt.

March said: 'Cocker, you deserve a medal for what you did a short time ago. Jack, 'ere, told me about it. Only if you'd rather we kept it to ourselves, we won't say a word. All the best, old mate, whatever you're plannin'. I reckon you'll make it back to U.K.'

'Sure, that goes for me, too, Britwell,' Profitt added. He was blinking rapidly

242

and making a big fist with his good arm. 'And look after that bit of stuff of yours. She's real pretty. Too good to be left around 'ere, if you asks me.'

Britwell thanked them, grabbed his things and went off down the stairs again. He almost collided with Christina, who was back in her track suit. Dr Geijssen moved heavily along behind her, coming from the operating theatre. He was peeling off rubber gloves and removing his round white hat like an automaton.

In stilted English, he said: 'You are just leaving? It had to be so.' Christina gave him a hug. The doctor slowly released himself. 'I'm sorry to say the English officer, Captain Birks, has just died. I did all I could.'

15

Jan van Vliet had lots to say about the action at the small hospital, but the tired authorities there would have none of his explanations. He was shooed off towards the river, warned to get all the German bodies away from the vicinity and bluntly asked not to return. Between them, Britwell and Christina hauled him away when he insisted upon going back to report the hamlet clear of the enemy's dead.

After that, Jan drew Britwell away on a foraging expedition along the southern bank of the Lower Rhine, looking for British supply drop canisters which had drifted clear of the allied positions. It soon became clear that Jan was better at it than the fair Briton, but the redhead, who expended a great deal more energy in climbing trees and telegraph poles to cut down the stray canisters, took the exercise all in good part and did not grumble.

Some forty minutes later, Christina returned from a reconnaissance expedition into the rest of the hamlet. While she had been there, she was told how the doctors would get rid of the injured German officer whom Britwell had knocked out of the window. The old orderly, who was far more talkative than the doctors, explained that they would check him over, patch him up and give him a goodly shot of dope before placing him in a row boat and floating him off down the river.

On hearing this from Christina, Britwell reacted in the same way that she had done earlier: and was assured in the same way. The German would be some distance away before his countrymen found him. Moreover, he would not be able to give information about the place where he had suffered until his head was clear of the morphia. And by that time, a great deal of change might well have taken place on both sides of the river.

Between noon and one in the afternoon, the trio were reclining on short grass between trees some fifty yards back from the river bank, taking a picnic lunch which Christina had managed to acquire back in Broek.

Across the river to the north, the devastating sounds of battle fluctuated but never ceased. It was clear to all three of them without discussion that the perimeter of the British airborne forces was being squeezed in an all-out attempt to force a surrender before the conventional land forces coming up the corridor were close enough to relieve them.

A point of discussion, however, which the trio could not put aside much longer concerned their future movements. Britwell was distressed. He knew Jan to be a wild man, reckless to the point of foolhardiness, who by his total involvement might very likely endanger Christina's life at any time.

Having found her brother, and assured herself that whatever he had done in the way of collusion, or pretended collusion with the enemy, he was now fighting hard for the Netherlands and the allied cause, Christina had to think ahead.

'We can't stay here, can we, Harry?' the

girl remarked, as they finished the food.

'That much is certain, Chrissy. I don't like to see you in danger but you are a Dutchwoman. Now you've found Jan, I'd like to know what you want to do next. My aim is selfish. To see you out of Holland, fit and well. As soon as possible.'

Jan stared at him, round-eyed and frankly surprised at the apparent depth of feeling between Britwell and his sister. Before answering, Christina rolled towards the Englishman and ducked her head under his left arm, laying it against his chest.

'What do you say, Jan?'

The big fellow shrugged. 'If you aren't planning to go south towards safety, we can go north. Into the British area. *Der Kessel*, as the Germans call it. We can call on our aunt and get information about our parents. I don't think your mother will be in Utrecht. And father will have gone to earth, in any case, since the railways are on total strike.'

Britwell was hooked on the German expression, *der Kessel*. 'The Cauldron.' He thought: Might as well call it the cauldron of death. Fancy a lovesick man having to follow his truelove into such a lethal spot when the alternatives were numerous.

He also had time to reflect upon the attitude of his sweetheart and her brother after their country had been occupied for so long. Both seemed concerned, and yet not vitally so about the risks being run by their closest blood relations in *der Kessel*. He wondered if he would ever get the girl out alive and whether their romance would be allowed by the war to flourish.

Christina said: 'Harry, I have made up my mind. It is too soon to turn for the south and safety. We will cross the river, and visit our aunt, my father's sister. Cora van Vliet. She was widowed in the first World War. Nothing will shift her, if she is still alive. She will have news of the other relations. I think we should cross over quite soon. Do you agree?'

Britwell nodded. Jan turned his head aside to hide a frown. He murmured: 'Cora van Vliet Neeskens.' The tone of his voice suggested that Mevrouw van Vliet Neeskens was a woman who knew how to handle a reckless and self-willed nephew.

Five minutes later, they were on their feet and moving nearer the water and up-stream in the direction of the northern settlement of Heveadorp. An old ferry plied between Heveadorp and the out-skirts of Driel, which was further east than Broek, their last visiting place.

All the while they walked the banks they were aware of the titanic struggle to the north. Mortar bombs cracked with a shattering boom against the ear-drums, even at that distance. The rattle and clatter of tracks, mostly driving German tanks and SP guns around the shrinking British citadel, were scarcely ever silent.

Bren guns, 6 inch anti-tank guns, Piats and machine-guns, both British and German, blazed away as though there was sufficient ammunition about to go on forever. Every now and then, the sinister hissing noise produced by a flame-thrower punctured the general cacophony, and many of the shells belched into the ruins by the dreaded *Konigstiger* tanks (recently arrived as rein-forcements from the east) were phosphorus projectiles calculated to cause fires as well as immediate destruction.

Britwell saw, heard and smelled enough to appal him long before he arrived in the area of the Heveadorp ferry opposite Driel. Hidden behind a low wall, he stared long and hard at the nearest action going on across the broad, fast-flowing river.

On high ground to westward across the Rhine a useful German battery was aiming shells along the south side of the British held territory. Jan explained that the settlement on the high ground was called Westerbouwing, and that one or two determined men ought to be able to sneak up there at night and spike the whole of the guns without difficulty.

Christina gave him a healthy tongue-lashing. 'Stop boasting, you fool, and think how we should get across now. You, you spend too much of your time looking too far ahead!'

In a temper, Jan set his teeth till his jaw muscles stood out to a remarkable degree, but Christina, who knew him well, stared him out and he relaxed, backed down and gave his attention to the problem of crossing over.

'The ferry is at the other side. At this moment, no one is using it, and there are no troops close to it. Neither British nor German. It's my belief we've only to set in motion the engine which works the cable controlling it, and it will come across to fetch us. Would you like to bet on it?'

Britwell grinned and shook his head. Christina showed signs of mounting impatience. Jan desisted. He asked the other two to stay where they were in cover while he himself crawled to the shed where the engine controls were housed. The door was difficult to open, but he managed it and dived through it, hauling it closed again shortly afterwards.

The engine started and stopped a time or two, and then worked efficiently. At the other side of the river, there were sounds which suggested mooring ropes were parting. The broad, low-built ferryboat started to come across the foaming waterway propelled by the steel cable attachments. Jan threw open the door, stuck out his arm and put up a big thumb, gesturing to the other two about his success.

His thumb instantly became a target. Two Spandaus fired from the slope below Westerbouing hosed streams of bullets at him. He dived back into the shed. Christina clutched Britwell, her heart pounding. She thought that Jan's end was in sight.

Their nerves received another pounding as a small battery which had been idle so far started to drop shells in the direction of the ferry. A lesser shell demolished the shed about Jan's ears. The ferry made progress, was about one third of the way across the river when the first shell hit it. Two near misses made the cable twist and thresh about. One of the shells in the next salvo hit it squarely midships, and a small fire started. Other guns took up the awful cacophony. The cables ceased to function. The fire spread, and there was an explosion which capped every item so far. Already low in the water, the ancient water bus began to swing away from its usual route, heading bows on downstream, a sad smoking wreck which had served the locals in their everyday life for many years.

Jan chose an early time to withdraw from the demolished shed. Partially screened by the smoking mass in mid-river, he rolled clear and sprinted for the low protective walling. Wooden splinters clung to his tunic and were in his hair. A smear of oil had darkened one side of his face.

Britwell for once adopted a mocking tone. 'Well, Jan, you always do things in style, and that's a fact. You'll always be able to say you were in at the death of the ferry.'

The girl squeezed his hand to make him desist. Jan looked alternately angry and crestfallen.

★   ★   ★

One hour later, they were back in the same area. Jan had found a rowing boat. He wanted to row his sister and Britwell over in it at approximately the same spot where the ferry had operated. He argued that the Germans would not expect anyone to attempt a crossing at the scene of so recent a disaster.

Britwell protested that if his reasoning was wrong, it could prove costly. They could lose their lives in one swift burst of concentrated automatic fire. In fact, he argued even further, suggesting that the Germans might be sending a party down to the wharf on the north side to separate the British from the river.

A rather unusual falling off in German gunfire had an effect upon their arguing. By this time, they had heard so much deafening artillery and tank fire that they could almost guess at the perimeter of the British territory. Now, it seemed that every gun in the ring of steel threatening the perimeter had stopped firing. Lack of ammunition could not have caused it. Clearly, something was on.

Jan, the great opportunist, wanted to take advantage of it. The lovers were slow to convince. He grabbed each of them by an arm, and talked convincingly, suggesting that further east a crossing would be more foolhardy, and that this might be their last chance before nightfall.

Still harbouring reservations in the mind, Britwell lowered the girl into the boat and dropped in beside her. Every second, the Englishman expected *the* lethal burst of tracer shells to hurtle towards them and terminate his romance: eliminate them both. But it failed to come. Jan pushed heartily with an oar, leapt into the boat himself, and scrambled into the oarsman's seat. As soon as he was there, he worked the oars with the strength of three men, or so it appeared to those dependent upon him.

He had to fight the current all the way. Britwell helped by keeping the rudder part way over. Progress was slow, which added to the tension but gradually the north bank came nearer, and Jan's confidence mounted as his breathing grew laborious. He finished the last twenty yards by operating the oars alternately, instead of together. Such was the improved speed near the bank that Britwell had great difficulty in preventing its ramming the wharf.

Britwell tied it up, eyed the nearest buildings back from the wharf, and coaxed Christina up the moss-covered steps built into the wall. Jan came up more slowly, blowing like a veteran walrus and carrying all their gear. Still troubled by the silent guns, they made for a small cottage which had lost its roof.

As their breathing eased, so they heard the first indistinct sounds of approaching aircraft. At their backs, it was as if both sides were listening for planes. And this was true. The distant hum grew louder, and still louder. Within three minutes the first of the German batteries on the east side of the British perimeter was blasting skyward.

The shells were aimed in patterned salvoes far wide of the British lines. In fact, they were decorating the sky with grey puffs east of Driel, back from the south bank: not far from the territory traversed earlier that day by the three comrades. Other batteries joined in, all significantly around the British perimeter and all firing into the sky west and south of Driel. The first wave of bulky troop transports must have looked good to the beleaguered Britons inside the ring, but the relief must have been tempered by other feelings connected with the hostile reception. All around the planes, shells burst and streams of brightly coloured tracer slanted towards them in curving, deceptively fast-moving arcs.

Nine planes were in view by the time the first of the parachutists sprang clear of the jumping doors and began to plummet down from some five hundred feet towards the troubled earth beneath. One of the second trio of planes suffered a direct hit. Flames licked around the fuselage aft of the cockpit and while the jumpers were still leaping clear.

The scene appeared to grow larger to the watchers with their straining upturned faces. Here and there, the tracer bullets linked up with men whose parachutes had blossomed, but others continued to float towards the earth in ever increasing numbers, filling the grey-pocked sky with bright colours of silk and grim-faced men in trim jumping smocks.

Earlier that day, it had been the intention of the planners to 'drop' the Polish Parachute Brigade on the polder south of Arnhem, but since it was now known that the bridge was in German hands, their venue had been changed to the country east of Driel, a position easily identifiable for incoming transport pilots on account of a prominent church spire in Driel itself.

As Britwell cringed with his arms pinning Christina from the rear, the chancy, costly air to ground warfare went on, and the correspondent's thoughts were abruptly thrown back to that frustrating uncertain time when he had tried all he knew to get himself trained sufficiently well to come to Holland by plane and parachute.

Jan's rugged face reflected many facets of the developing action. Grimaces for damaged planes and riddled parachutists: grim smiles for clusters of men whose parachutes had sunk below the line of their vision. Christina's voice sounded husky as she spoke.

'Why do you suppose they dropped them south of the river, Harry?'

Britwell's grip around her shoulders eased. 'To think I tried to get them to let me parachute into Holland. I might have been riddled. What? What were you saying? Oh, yes. I suppose they dropped them there to make some sort of link with the troops coming up from the south. Yes, that's seems probable!'

'But there would have had to be a proper link up with the other men who came earlier,' Jan argued.

'Yes, I think you are both right,' Christina yelled, above the din. 'They would have expected to use the ferry. I believe now the Bosches must have known they were coming. That's why it was being so closely watched when we tried to use it.'

Jan rose to his feet. 'They'll still get across. It isn't all that difficult.'

Big Jan led them away in search of Aunt Cora's cottage. No one interfered with them. The German gunners were concentrating upon the planes and parachutists. Their infiltraters had ceased operations for a time. The British, meanwhile, were taking a breather and conserving their dwindling supplies of ammunition. Slowly and carefully, they negotiated the heaps of rubble, some of them smoking. Quite a time was taken in covering a relatively short distance. At the end of it, there was disappointment and shock.

Cora's cottage was one of the inner ones of a terrace of four. Since the fighting had begun, the two middle cottages had been blasted to ground level. Heaps of shattered stone and smashed tiles covered what was once the ground floor of the snug dwelling.

Christina winced and her face puckered when she saw it.

Jan said: 'That seems to be it, sis. Don't weaken in front of the foreigner. You know how she was. Wouldn't leave home for Hitler himself.'

Christina was sobbing in Britwell's arms. The two men glared at each other. This time the big Dutchman looked away first. He knew that he had spoken without thinking, and that his words had been inappropriate. He bent to the bag of weapons he had been carrying and began to take them out of their coverings.

'We'll need to contact some British

commander, and do what we can,' Jan mumbled, as the general cacophony of sound began to fade.

'That goes without saying,' Britwell replied. 'But Christina needs a minute or two to recover.'

16

Noordelden. A small select hamlet south of the 'Cauldron' and really on the outskirts of Oosterbeek, the town which had become the heart of the paratroopers' resistance. By the time the van Vliets and Britwell arrived on the north side of the river Noordelden had been suffering for several days during most of the hours of daylight, on account of its close proximity to the river. Clearly, the Germans' intention was to try and force a wedge along the northern river bank to prevent allied passage across the waterway.

There were only a few streets in the hamlet, even before the artillery got at it. Now, the population appeared to be nil. One could only suppose that the survivors had moved on to less dangerous parts: the woods to the north, or elsewhere.

The trio were still puzzling about the missing population when they stumbled upon the dilapidated headquarters of the nearest British unit; in the south-west sector between Oosterbeek Laag and Heveadorp. This was controlled by two companies of the Border Regiment at the time.

A tired major with dark rings under his eyes and a painful leg wound did not take kindly to Jan's description of their recent adventures. This officer promptly told the voluble Dutchman to shut up, and required Britwell and Christina to answer a few questions.

While they were questioned as to their bona fides, two other officers, an N.C.O. and one other rank all showed signs of dropping off to sleep in the close atmosphere of the partially demolished house. Eventually, the major toppled a few inches over the deal table and unluckily banged his wounded leg. This brought the interrogation to a halt.

'Oh, all right, damn it! Two of you have worked with the Resistance and the other came in with the Yanks as a war correspondent. If you're what you say you are, for goodness' sake prove it. Get out and get busy. You, van Vliet, there's a Polish officer engaged for liaison somewhere around here. He's dying to cross the Lower Rhine with information for the Polish Parachute Brigade which dropped on the other side this afternoon. See the officer gets across, and then find something useful to do!'

In spite of the officer's rather wearing tone of voice, Jan took his orders without demur and ducked out after banging his head on a low beam. He did not act as though the war was likely to come between himself and his sister in the next day or two.

'Miss van Vliet, there's a Regimental Aid Post somewhere east of here in what's left of a private house. Perhaps you would go along there and see what you can do to help out. The staff are practically staggering with fatigue. Britwell could make himself useful there, too. There's plenty of work, even for non-combatants.'

Britwell smiled briefly and grimly, but did not say anything about his earlier involvements. He had nothing more in mind than keeping Christina in sight and being generally useful. He had a feeling that the fate of himself and his two Dutch comrades had already been decided.

The going was hazardous on the way to the Regimental Aid Post, but the volunteers made it across the rubbled streets, through the parts rendered hazardous by snipers without mishap in about ten minutes. Christina's clear incisive voice, speaking of her experience and insisting upon helping straight away soon had them established. The wounded were in all the bedrooms, in two attics, on the landing and in almost every other space above ground level. The drugs were getting low, the staff terribly tired and the steady intake of new casualties was taking a terrible toll of those who cared.

Christina stripped off her track suit and got down to work at once. Britwell could see dirty heavy jobs all around him. Where the nurses and doctors did not speak English, he simply studied what they were doing and guessed their requirements. At first, the Englishman had a terrific sense of achievement as he toiled in the inadequate spaces, hearing the rattle and clatter of weapons beyond the building and the occasional fall of masonry. Gradually, the hours moved along towards midnight. Clearly, the soldiers were tired enough to ease up a bit, but there was no let up possible for the medical workers.

This was going to be an all night session at the Post, and the work was absorbing all the energy of the newcomers. At times, Britwell almost regretted having come along. He could see that his beautiful auburn-haired sweetheart was grieving over something, and he correctly assumed her mood had to do with the missing aunt.

The work went on, with Britwell promoted to jobs like bed-making and routine attendance on patients.

* * *

During the same hours, Jan escorted the Polish officer down to the river, where he explained in detail how best to swim across the current and where to emerge. Having done this, and being short of

something to do, he acted upon something the Pole had told him and went on
a private forage, seeking out water which
was becoming something of a problem,
especially for the British. Rumour had it
that many of the pumps and wells were
covered by snipers. This impressed Jan
who, therefore, determined to collect his
water in small amounts with a little added
excitement. In fact, he collected the water
canteens of the dead. He was mindful of
possible booby traps, but he found none.

Sometimes, in his meandering prowl,
he found himself 'lifting' the water bottle
of a man in a deep sleep, rather than
dead. On an occasion like this, a British
soldier would receive an apology and a
friendly poke in the ribs, whereas a
Panzer grenadier would most probably
receive a bayonet thrust in a vital part,
which meant he did not require his water
any more.

Clattering a lot, Jan found his way back
to the local H.Q. where he had started
and turned over part of his load. He then
asked the way to the Aid Post where his
friends had gone and took the rest of his

loot to them. Around midnight, he went suddenly tired and curled up out of doors at the back behind a coal bunker.

He would not have slept at all had he known that it was planned for the Polish parachutists on the south side of the river to make a crossing in small collapsible boats provided by the garrison of *der Kessel*. However, he did not miss the action because the Germans infiltrated along part of the northern river bank and prevented the British garrison from getting the boats to the water.

⋆ ⋆ ⋆

Friday dawn was a cold, grey misty affair. In fact, the chill in the atmosphere awoke Jan van Vliet at an early hour and drove him indoors where he began to fetch and carry for the nurses before washing himself in a minimal amount of water. Britwell was awakened by Jan who was whistling to himself as he dried off with a towel. The latter gave the impression that this crucial day was as mundane as any other, so casual was his approach to another day of crisis. Britwell rose stiffly from his pre-stained mattress stretched out on a corridor and wondered what there was to whistle about. In spite of everything the medical team had done the scent of wounds and death was beginning to permeate the building.

Outside, the rain began to fall quite heavily. On all sides, the guns had started up again. Tiger tanks and other iron-clads of a smaller calibre were working their way into the shrinking British lines and creating havoc, as before. The SP guns were also active. Phosphorus shells, mortar bombs and high explosives peppered the *Cauldron*, while infiltrating infantry sniped at and hindered the tired defenders of the many sectors.

Concerted attacks were made first against one unit and flank, and then against another. Loud-mouthed Germans called out in English for the Tommies to surrender, that they had fought well and that further resistance was useless.

Men cursed and swore and wished they had a sufficiency of weapons and ample ammunition to silence the voices and the guns without delay. Meanwhile, their innards suffered. Earlier in the week, there had been pork and venison to eat on occasion, or worthwhile stores taken from cupboards of abandoned houses. Now, after five days the diet was falling off. The beleaguered natives had nothing to offer the sky soldiers. In the trenches, the diet amounted to sardines, biscuits and boiled sweets washed down by a small amount of water. After that, action without let-up and a mounting thirst. Christina appeared from her cot in a loft and ran up and down stairs a couple of times while Jan was explaining to Britwell what their food consisted of.

Christina in a short skirt, white blouse and plimsolls, taking the steps two at a time on her long lithe sunburned legs, was a sight to see, especially with her hair billowing out behind her. She had only slept for three hours and yet she radiated health for all who regarded her.

With his eyes on the girl, Britwell learned that the soup was made from tulips. They had also figured in some respect in the making of the biscuits. For extra measure, Jan — who had a phenom-enal appetite — produced a handful of tulip bulbs which he had found in his travels. Britwell sampled a couple, hoping that his stomach would not protest at a later time.

Christina joined them for a few minutes, munching biscuits and enjoying their company before the vital chores of the day set them apart.

She said: 'One of the doctors heard that the Poles who landed near Driel should have crossed over last night, but the Germans were harassing the British along the north bank and they were not able to get down there with the small boats. So the Poles did not come. What do you think they'll do, Harry?'

Britwell made an effort to seem cheerful. 'Obviously, they will try again. Perhaps tonight. If not, it might be necessary to withdraw the British to the south bank. If they aren't in touch with the bridge there's no point in staying. If they were stronger, it would be different. I feel they've caused a heap of suffering for the local people, perhaps to no avail.'

Jan snorted, but Christina's blue eyes

271

mirrored pain. She gripped Britwell's arm, looked directly into his eyes, and half-brother Jan felt cut out again. Almost at the same time, there was a dull clang out at the back. Falling splinters from SP shells had holed the emergency water tank. The contents, down to a few inches, spilled out on to the surrounding earth causing short-lived consternation among the staff.

The senior doctor pointed out that rust and dirt had got into the tank and that it was dangerous to drink without boiling. If the Post was to survive as an efficient unit, something had to be done that day to bring cleaner water in from elsewhere in large quantities.

Jan accepted the assignment without demur, and Britwell elected to assist him, primarily because it was such a vital necessity and also because the over-crowded state of the Aid Post was giving him claustrophobia.

★ ★ ★

By ten a.m., the two had done most of the difficult chores at the Post, and they parted with a number of water bottles and buckets to do what they could about getting them filled. The nearest pump was some sixty yards away. Assisted by the rain and the minute directions of an old Dutch nurse, they worked their way into the low-walled garden where the pump was located. All went well for perhaps five minutes, except that the pump handle creaked rather ominously and in the near-silence between reverberating explosions its groaning got on their nerves.

When all the water bottles and receptacles except one were filled, Jan had the misfortune to clatter the empty one on the cobbles. At once, Britwell stiffened. Jan knew no fear, but if he had a sixth sense, it was working for him then.

'Quick, Harry, over the wall and crawl along the other side!'

Britwell grabbed what he took to be half the gear and hopped over the wall. Jan sprawled across him with the rest just as an ominous noise occurred at the base of the pump. Two or three seconds later, a stick grenade exploded in a terrific cone of white light tinged with red. Cobbles and earth flew in all directions, and the fate of the pump was a matter for speculation.

Ten minutes later, in spite of their narrow escape, the two water carriers reported back to the Post, and were thankfully received by a doctor and Christina, both of whom feared that they had lost their lives in the latest venture.

Jan strutted up and down, full of vigour and feeling ten feet high as a result of the exploit. He wanted to undertake a further task, at a greater distance. The nearest well of any size, he was given to understand, was between Oosterbeek Laag and Noordelden, where Aunt Cora had lived.

The bearded doctor explained: 'Many people have lost their lives near the well, because the buildings round about it have been damaged and it is possible for snipers to keep it covered from some distance away. But the well water is good. Maybe the situation will change soon, so that it can be used again!'

Christina had gone back to her duties. Only the doctor was there to witness Big

Jan's growing enthusiasm. Presently, an army doctor came along in a jeep with his orderly and took the Dutch doctor indoors. Jan was torn between asking for an eleven o'clock snack and going straight over to the well and getting to work. Britwell delayed him long enough to collect most of the more suitable utensils for water carrying and noted that he was bringing along with him all available weapons of war.

'You think we might have to fight for the well water, Jan?' Britwell asked calmly.

Big Jan shrugged and grinned. 'Things aren't getting any easier, Harry. You saw how it was at the pump. Besides, a bit of sport adds excitement to a boring chore, don't you think?'

'For goodness' sake, Jan, take it seriously! If not for your own sake, for Christina's. This sort of caper isn't my idea of sport. We want a lot of luck to succeed where others have died. We might not even make it to the place!'

The sudden flash of anger made the Dutchman raise his brows.

'All right, then. No funny business. We

set out to outwit the Germans, right? And if any of them get in our way, we have to do something about it. After all, *they* drink. We *might* have to fight them for the water. So let's go.'

Fifteen minutes of cautiously probing one wrecked street after another brought them reasonably close to the patch of green belt between one half of a terrace of houses and the other. Caution paid off then. Still fifty yards away, Jan pointed to a brick gable end that had lost most of the side walls which had adjoined it.

'From the top of there, we can see right across into the well yard, and also take stock of the surroundings. How about a short climb?'

Britwell squinted up at the structure and had his doubts about whether it would support their combined weight, but the clattering tracks of a German SP gun moving along the next street further north in an easterly direction made them jump for cover into the battered shell of the house.

'I could maybe stop that gun for good with a grenade,' Jan announced, as he fumbled in his sack of war materials. 'That would be something, wouldn't it?'

'No, it wouldn't. Even if you succeeded, you'd be drawing attention to the street where the well is. And most likely we'd never be able to get near after that.'

Jan backed off, impressed by the argument. 'There speaks the voice of a sober-minded Englishman. So, we climb, instead.'

Using the empty frame of a window in the gable wall, he was soon some eight feet off the ground. Somehow gripping the crenellated edge of crumbled brick, Jan reached down and hauled Britwell up after him. Presently, some twenty feet above rubble level, the two men studied the next street north, where the well yard was.

It was not so much a yard as a garden with a well in it. The crew of SP gunners stopped there deliberately and brought up a bucket which clattered against the well sides. Jan yearned to take offensive action against them, but having once desisted on his partner's advice, he held himself back. Five minutes later, the SP gun wheezed into life and moved off.

'I'm sure there's a German or two in the roofless house to the left of the well yard,' Jan opined.

'There's a German or two almost everywhere, amigo,' Britwell replied morosely.

It was tiring, clinging to the top of that partially demolished gable end, but another few minutes of patient observation paid off. Someone in the roofless house tossed a match stalk out of the window. It burned briefly before the breeze put it out. Jan chuckled, and intimated that Fritz might be smoking his last cigarette.

He added: 'That well garden looks very interesting to me. Before the Germans became so numerous, somebody dug a long open trench the full length of it from west to east, just this side of the well itself. That'll come in useful. We can crawl along it.'

'I begin to see what you intend,' Britwell admitted, his face screwed up in deep speculation. 'You intend to get the better of the smoker, then crawl up the trench to the well, and maybe crawl all the way back again.'

'Something like that,' Jan agreed, warming to the coming move. 'You see those two screening side-walls, one west and one east of the well? We can use them to give us protection while we do the actual filling. How we come out, though. That's a matter for conjecture. We might have trouble, but we know the risk is worthwhile. So let's not delay any longer, eh?'

Britwell's arms were shaking with the physical effort of clinging to the rough brickwork, and he was doubly pleased about scrambling back to earth level again. As soon as he was down below, the war correspondent used the binoculars on the street to the north which separated them from the terraced houses and the well. What he saw, or failed to see, confirmed his earlier impression: if anyone lived in the buildings between, it was below ground, and native Dutch people, rather than hiding infiltrators. If there were other snipers with the well under observation, the chances were they were seeing it from an easterly direction.

★   ★   ★

As a team, Harry Britwell and Jan van Vliet worked well.

Ten minutes after reaching the ground again, they put their strategy into operation. First of all, exercising all possible stealth, Britwell slipped across the rubbled road to the building directly north. He went in through a window gap, took his time in crossing the pitted floor and eventually found himself in a position to study the next building — the key one — through a holed wall in a kneeling position. It was dark in the interior. The only sign of movement was the gentle flapping of leaves on slim branches: the plant was a creeper type attached to the crumbled wall.

Suddenly, the Englishman felt cool and confident. While he was marvelling at the steadiness of his nerves, van Vliet, the former hammer thrower and shot putter, went into action. First one and then another grenade sailed through the air in a gentle arc towards the building Britwell was observing.

The first one narrowly missed the window opening and bounced back into the street, giving him a shock. He crouched down, tensed up and awaiting the explosion, expecting it to hit his hideout rather than the other.

In the meantime, the second grenade sailed through the window at which it was aimed, narrowly missed a reclining sniper stretched out below it, and erupted right on time. The wooden floor was demolished over a large area. Rubble which had been lying on it, cascaded down into the basement. The sniper died. The whole of the remaining structure was filled with smoke. Furthermore, an end window on the well side, one which had been bricked up for a few years, lost its filling and gave a clear view of the vital area beyond it. In knocking out a couple of bricks for observation purposes, the sniper had weakened the filling bricks and precipitated the falling out of the rest.

'Britwell, what are you waiting for?'

Big Jan's voice sounded hoarse and angry. Britwell at once stood up, in spite of his not having heard the other grenade go off. There was only dust, smoke and debris in the street on the north side and no sign of the unexploded grenade. Was it a dud?

The second explosion was overdue. That much was clear. He was just turning in the direction of the Dutchman when the first of several empty water containers hurtled through the window and almost knocked him on his back. He caught it, an Army 'dixie', by springing about and trapping it in his arms.

As he caught the second, a huge Dutch pot, heavy enough for boiling purposes, van Vliet called again.

'Keep them coming, Jan,' Britwell called back. 'Your second shot was a good one!'

Some three minutes later, upwards of a dozen containers had been tossed through the window and somehow trapped by the breathless Englishman. Jan followed the last one, entering with a leaping forward roll and coming to his feet with a Schmeisser automatic somehow still in his grasp and undischarged.

For a few seconds, the two of them

studied the scene to the north speculatively. No sign of the enemy. Only dust, debris and so on. The explosion sounds had faded to nothing and the more distant background noises occasioned by sharp automatic and small arms clashes appeared to grow louder. Neither were put off.

'All right, partner?' Jan asked, when he had recovered his breath. 'I'm on my way. Give me cover, and then sling over the utensils! There's still some smoke and dust about.'

Jan used the door this time, racing across the open space for the other building at a speed which would have surprised Christina. He dived through the open window, uttered a brief roar of disgust as he disappeared from sight and left Britwell ill-at-ease and with doubts mounting in the mind.

No sign of anyone prowling the streets. Time to get moving with the water containers. Discarding his Schmeisser, the Englishman hurled a big container with all his strength. He had played some cricket in peacetime, and he did not want to be shown up by his partner's throwing skill.

The container briefly caught a flash in the bleak autumn sun before disappearing through the window and prompting another roar of disgust from within. Britwell could only conclude that he had somehow struck his partner.

'Everything all right?'

'Keep them coming!' Jan replied brusquely.

Britwell continued the action. Only one receptacle was off target. That one clattered off the outside wall. All the others disappeared from view and no other setbacks occurred. The breathless fair man intimated that he was about to run over, and was surprised to get an immediate response.

'Count ten before you come. Don't come through the window with too much force! Floor missing!'

Still breathing hard, and feeling that their luck could not last out much longer, Britwell grabbed his weapon and vaulted over the sill. He felt naked as he raced across the rubble, bending sharply to recover the can en route, and then rolled over the sill of the other building.

In spite of the warning, his impetus carried him too far forward. He toppled over the opening in the floor, and was caught half way through a somersault by Jan, who had been in the act of trying on a German tunic, the property of his recent victim.

Jan ripped out a few choice and pithy Dutch swear words before hoisting Britwell above him and holding him up long enough to clutch the holed floor and swing himself clear. Britwell moved to the windows: the one giving on to the street, and then the other which commanded a view of the well. All clear, for the moment.

Jan leapt upwards, and for his effort failed to make it. His gripping hands merely ripped away splinters of wood, dropping him back where he had come from. He cursed again, remarked that Fritz (the dead man) did not help by staring all the time, and made a second effort.

This time he leapt higher. Britwell was

able to grip the back of the German belt and steady him when he started to slide. After a struggle lasting a minute, they knelt together, side by side, studying the well yard and the territory beyond.

'Do you think anyone will spot us before we get the cans filled?' Britwell asked, over Jan's shoulder.

The Dutchman sniffed. 'I think it is very likely. The fortunes of war, you know, old man. If they do, we'll simply have to act first.'

Jan rose to his feet in cover. He took off the German tunic, rolled it up and stuffed it with a German forage cap inside his old brown combat jacket. He indicated a roll of strong string which he had found, and at once the two of them started to fasten the containers together about a yard apart.

'You want to go first, this time, Harry?'

Britwell swallowed hard. 'If you like, Jan. I'm getting to be fatalistic about this unreal bit of the war. I'll get into that trench as soon as you say. Just so long as I see your red head coming along behind me without too long a delay, all will be well.'

The two of them were moved to show a bit of emotion. They shook hands, and Jan made a mental note to look after Harry for Christina's sake. He felt that his sister would never forgive him if anything serious happened to this unsoldierly Englishman who was supposed to write about the war and so often found himself involved.

Britwell scraped his chest going over the sill into the garden. He lowered himself into the trench and at once started to worm his way along it. He had with him the end of the string. As soon as it appeared to tighten, he tugged it twice, received a signal in return and glanced back in time to see Jan lob the first container over the sill and into the trench. It was at this stage that the awful tension knotted Britwell's chest and made him wonder just how much time would have to elapse before they could breathe easily again. Crawling along like a newt, his muscles began to ache. He began to have an inkling of what it was really like for parachutists and glider men to fight night and day without any possibility of a let-up and with constantly changing circumstances and pressures.

He drew the canisters after him, paused for breath and took a cautious look around. The gable beyond the garden patch was intact, except that the windows had been blown in. The buildings in the street which they had crossed had a dead look. In contrast, a blackbird flew over him. It perched briefly on the narrow tiled roof above the well and flew on again. Distantly, a dog barked. That made him think. What was left of a dog's world in this holocaust?

Jan snapped his fingers and left the building like a trooper in a peacetime recruiting advertisement. This time he dropped into the trench without difficulty. They had all the containers between them. Britwell curled himself up and hauled until they were as far along as he could manage. He then wrapped the free length around his arm like a woman with a clothes line, signalled that he was ready to move on and braced himself for the effort.

Up and out, paying out the line as he

raced for the shelter of the side wall. He was almost there before he noticed the long silver canister standing beside the well, mounted on a trolley with rubber tyres. Others had been along earlier and maybe filled the torpedo-shaped container, but they had not been able to get away again with their precious booty.

Jan rose out of the trench, holding up the last three canisters. Britwell hauled and in a few seconds they were crouched behind the well-side wall on the west side; protected by four feet of shrapnel-pitted and bullet-chipped bricks. And still intact . . .

The trolley canister was full. That was lucky, if they could only take it away with them. After that, it was a case of filling their containers with all haste. Jan's neck hairs were prickling. He had a feeling they were due for company. Britwell read his mood, left the Dutchman to do the guarding and himself worked the handle which controlled the bucket.

Perspiration streamed from him. He lost count of the number of times he hauled the bucket to the top and stared at its moss-covered outer rim. He kicked one of the oval-shaped containers and that set his nerves jangling.

'Get down!' Jan ordered.

Britwell dropped flat, in a prone position. The ominous patter of a bouncing stick bomb brought the Englishman out in cold perspiration all over. Not so his partner. Van Vliet leapt forward, grabbed it in motion and hurled it towards the trees bulking out beyond the houses to the south-east. It exploded in mid-air half way between the well and the trees, blasting their ear drums and disconcerting the thrower and others.

'What now, Jan?'

'It's time for a bit of play-acting, chum. You crawl round to the other side, take shelter behind the other wall. You're going to be my prisoner, but when you stand up have that Schmeisser close enough for a quick grab. We have trouble on two fronts!'

Britwell acted without further question. As soon as he had achieved the new position, he turned and marvelled at his friend's ingenuity. In the face of big trouble, he was about to pass himself off as a German non-commissioned officer. The Spandau operating from a fixed point high in an autumn-tinted tree opened up just before Jan was ready. He rolled to one side, fastened a couple of buttons on the tunic and rammed the forage cap on his head.

The Spandau burst was terminated. Bullets had glanced off the trolley canister and hit the wall, but no damage was done.

Jan shouted in German: '*Hold it! Hold your fire! This Englander is my prisoner!*'

To add weight to his words, he rose to his feet and ponderously waved his arm. His next words were addressed to Britwell, in German. While one palpitating second followed another without any further shooting from the trees, Britwell rose to his feet, his hands held high above his head. At this moment in time, his head was bare but his khaki combat jacket suggested a British paratrooper, even without flashes.

Jan stepped closer, digging him in the back with the muzzle of the Schmeisser.

'There's one bastard in the top window of that house and two snipers over in those trees. I'm going to try and get them to show themselves. After that, it'll be a matter of split second timing. You may have to deal with the fellow in the house. Spray him good and true, if you want to see my sister again. Okay?'

In German again, Jan renewed his shouting: 'All right, all right, this Englander is well supplied with cigarettes and he has a hip flask. I can supply you with water, the best, and a few titbits into the bargain. Who's interested? Come on now, show yourselves! I shan't ask a second time!'

Britwell's hands shook as he saw his comrade deliberately slipping two British hand grenades out of a pouch and into his hands. He was hearing and seeing responses from two places in the trees to the south-east when the tall trooper with eroded features appeared in the upper window of the gable end, directly ahead. The war correspondent's mouth dried out.

Jan was crouching for his first throw. Britwell recollected his words: '*Spray him good and true, if you want to see my sister again . . . .'* With his heart thumping, the fair man lowered his arms until his hands were resting on the top of the side wall. A second's pause and then he suddenly dropped down behind the wall, grabbed the automatic pistol and brought it up.

Jan gave a great heave and almost sighed as he summoned up a huge intake of air, prior to launching his second missile. The trooper in the window had tensed, opened his thin mouth and frowned. He appeared to be bringing up his weapon in slow motion. Britwell almost fired his Schmeisser as a direct reaction to the sudden explosion in the trees.

His first burst swung to one side, but as he fired the second he corrected the error and had the satisfaction of seeing the guard turn sharply on his heels, rise up to his full height and then disappear backwards.

The ear-shattering crash of the second grenade . . . The first sniper and the mangled remains of the Spandau were still spilling down to street level as the spreading circle of orange-tinged destruction scythed through the browning foliage, ripping down a wide tunnel of branches and filling the copse with smoke. Britwell, having perspired through his shirt, hurled himself in the direction of the trolley and began to attach the many containers to it with the string. Jan, meanwhile, fired a long burst into the copse, panning the barrel of his weapon around in a figure eight, just to make doubly sure there were no survivors.

'Great shooting, Harry,' he remarked hoarsely. 'Let's get all this gear together and then away. We'll take the street on the north side and hope for the best!'

So saying, the big Dutchman pulled off his forage cap and applied himself to the pressing chores. They pulled and coaxed the big trolley out of the well yard and started westward along the rubbled street with a strong feeling of relief promoting their waning energies.

Every corner, every intersection brought a tension which had Britwell near to choking. The Post was no more than fifty yards away when Jan surprised him once more.

'Can you manage it the rest of the way on your own, Harry?' he inquired urgently.

'Whatever for? Oh, yes, of course. All right! Don't stay away too long!'

With a broad grin on his face, Big Jan slipped away into a side street like some giant will-o-the-wisp. Britwell toiled on alone, drawn by the prospect of seeing Christina and getting a super welcome from the doctors and staff. To his surprise, he found no fewer than two doctors and three nurses out in the road.

He was to learn that in his absence, the British medical officer had managed to get the co-operation of a German M. O. operating outside *Der Kessel*. As a direct result, German ambulances had been making journeys between the Post and the biggest hospital in the area, removing the more seriously wounded British casualties. As soon as Britwell's clattering chariot was identified as the bearer of fresh water, he received a cheer and that lifted the tension in him for a time.

★   ★   ★

Britwell kissed Christina as she came hurrying out to help take indoors the invaluable water. She could feel the tension in him.

'You've been forced to kill again. Haven't you?'

He hugged her close, admitted that she had guessed the truth and omitted to excuse himself on the grounds that the fresh stock of water made it all right. She drew him into the immediate chores connected with water distribution. Gradually, his pulse went back to normal and he began to think that his part of the action was a small part to play in exchange for being reunited with his copper-haired sweetheart.

'Where's Jan?' the girl asked, twenty minutes later.

'He remembered some sort of an errand when we were nearly back again. I suppose he'll be along shortly.'

Standing between two beds, Christina gripped his hands and they both listened to the crack and crunch of mortar bombs, shells, and the whine of bullets, spelling out their messages of death. British guns were still firing from somewhere well to the south, but the German ring was reinforced to such an extent that only a colossal break-through from the south without delay could result in a stay of execution for the British who were denied the Arnhem bridge.

'I'll go and see if I can find him, if it will make you feel better, Chrissy,' he offered, wondering if Big Jan's days were numbered.

17

The search for Jan lasted for about ninety minutes. To Harry Britwell, however, it appeared to go on for a great deal longer than that. Prowling the southern borders of the threatened British perimeter was no sort of a quest for a man with poor nerves. At times, the odd mortar bomb came sailing over the ruins with no apparent target, other than that of destroying the morale of the defenders.

Now and then, grey-faced Dutch people, utterly weary after five days of incredible strain, ducked away from him as if his very presence was a threat to them and their dependents. Twice he almost lost his life when he blundered across the sights of German snipers, firing at near-maximum range.

Three or four times, his blundering search nearly brought a lethal burst from the small units of trigger-happy paratroopers who were fast running out of patience and a sense of proportion. He had to call out his name; proceed forward according to their very minute and detailed instructions.

On one occasion, a weary sergeant fell asleep when attempting to interrogate him in detail about the unconvincing way in which he had arrived in Holland. A second time it was nearly as bad. He was herded into the wreck of a tennis court with a few German prisoners. From there, he only managed to get his freedom by tongue-lashing a relief guard who was too far gone to worry whether he was a spy or not.

Not fifty yards from the spot where Aunt Cora's house had been, Britwell had his first break. He heard a hoarse, raucous voice singing snatches of the Dutch national anthem, and that could only be Jan. He found him jack-knifed over a low wall, striving with might and main to get out the last line or two without his voice going off-key. As Britwell approached, the big Dutchman stopped singing and began to laugh. His red face was upside down and only an inch or so off the wall which supported him.

In one hand, he had a short squat bottle which no doubt contained strong liquor.

'Jan van Vliet, you are the absolute bloody limit when it comes to unreliability! Where have you been in the last couple of hours? Don't answer that! I could have had myself blasted to shreds through trying to find you. You, who think you're some sort of a folk hero, you're nothing but a damned liability when the chips are down. No, don't try to explain. I couldn't stand to hear you. I've promised to get you back to the first aid post, and it looks as if I'll need all my strength, too.'

Jan straightened up with difficulty. The big fellow had some sort of idea which way to go, but his walking progress was so erratic that Britwell had to support him most of the time and prevent him from pitching on his head in the rubble. Between gasps, the Englishman wondered what sort of light-hearted relief had ended up with his former partner in this condition? Surely, he had not been entertained by any of the locals?

Jan's big booted feet hacked his legs. The strain grew every few yards. At last, one turn away from the Post, Big Jan started to sing again. His voice appeared to have grown in volume. One or two hiding locals noticed, and then came Christina to the rescue, running along in plimsolls, blouse and a short skirt.

The girl's great relief soon turned to concern for Britwell, whose face was almost grey with the effort he had made. Christina called for help, which came in the form of two elderly Dutchmen. Jan was taken away for a sponge down. Britwell, meanwhile, rightly or wrongly treated as the great water provider, received a small amount of water for washing purposes, and the offer of a small meal. After that, without wanting to, he fell asleep and was allowed to stay that way.

Later, Britwell was content to merely help in the Post and to keep Christina in sight as much as possible. Jan slept longer. He was given a small meal and a thorough tongue-lashing from his sister.

So guilty did he feel about turning up drunk that he went away in the dwindling hours of daylight, determined to work all night — if necessary — to make up for his lapse.

In his search for action and recognition, he made himself available to a bunch of Royal Engineers who had control of a number of rubber dinghies. These were taken down to the water's edge in spite of probing German guns. They were used to ferry the Poles from south to north in twos and threes.

The Germans knew what was on. Inevitably, there were casualties. Jan had a couple of dinghies destroyed under him, but he was still working hard at three o'clock in the morning when the Polish commanding officer called off the exercise. Some fifty Poles had been shipped across the Lower Rhine. Many others had lost their lives.

Saturday began with another grey, damp, clammy dawn thoroughly dowsed in drizzle. As the eastern sky brightened, Jan was tucked away somewhere sleeping like a babe. By contrast, Christina and

Britwell — both of whom had a secret fear that the British in Arnhem were surviving on borrowed time — arose early, and applied themselves efficiently and willingly to the everyday chores of the overworked Aid Post. It was only by working that Britwell's nerves stood up to the dawn chorus of guns that so buffeted the nervous systems of those who lived on.

⋆　⋆　⋆

After a meagre lunch, Jan became active again. He took Britwell with him to the river on a chancy mission which amounted to canister recovery. One more time the R.A.F. had flown over and dropped supplies. A goodly quantity had fallen straight into the hands of the encroaching Germans. Just a few had drifted across the Rhine, into territory held by the Poles, and even less appeared to have lost height finally over the river itself.

Searching for those by the river appeared to Jan as a worthwhile activity. Dodging and ducking through all kinds of cover to avoid snipers' bullets from the direction of Westerbouwing, the two ill-assorted comrades eventually arrived at that portion of the river bank which they had used on their first arrival.

Drifting towards them from upstream was a big metal canister, dragging behind it a flattened parachute and its cords. On seeing it, Big Jan enthused. It was moving steadily downstream, but he was equal to the challenge it presented, drifting as it was, twenty yards out from the bank. From a heap of rubble, he produced a long coil of rope with a grappling iron on the end.

'Money for old rope,' he remarked easily, with the butt of a German cigarette dangling from his lower lip. 'Just watch.'

He tossed the grappling iron into the tangled cords, arrested the progress of the canister and casually drew it ashore like a veteran fisherman hauling in a loaded net. Britwell would have taken the canister back to the Post, or one of the local military H.Q.s, but Jan was more ambitious. In following the line of the bank towards the east, they met with further success and an unexpected hazard.

Their second discovery, a swinging wicker hamper, was dangling from the gnarled branches of a towering, shrapnel-scarred tree. The two of them were staring up at it and wondering why no one else had seen it before them when two narrow canoes, each manned by four Germans with blackened faces, came skimming down the river, hugging the north bank.

Britwell just had time to call a warning and to draw his huge partner down out of sight. Jan had the good sense to take cover without pausing long enough to assess the strength of the opposition.

'Eight Krauts in two canoes, obviously bent on some little commando jaunt along this bank. What do you think about that?'

Jan grinned broadly. 'Who knows, Harry, they could be simply looking for canisters like we are. Keep your fingers crossed and they may come up by those steps just ahead of us.'

Britwell's stomach churned. Clearly,

the big Dutchman had already made up his mind to take on the entire platoon without seeking for assistance.

'Let the first boat load come up. You hit them from the side. I position myself further up the bank and hit the second crew before they disembark. All right?'

Britwell nodded and hoped so. He would have liked to suggest that the two canoes might come in useful, if they remained intact. Jan, however, had already moved away and, in any case, such a surmise on reflection smacked of over-confidence. The Englishman was a trifle surprised when the first canoe scraped the metal ring at the bottom of the stone steps, whereas his partner acted as though the whole thing had been preordained.

Their padded boots were light on the wet, slippery steps. Like ballet dancers they moved up, four athletic highly-strung men primed by pep pills and ready to wince at a shadow. The swinging wicker basket a few yards away affected them, one after the other. Recognising it, and knowing it for what it was seemed to steady their nerves.

A pebble shifted under Jan van Vliet's boot. At once, Britwell opened up with his machine-pistol from the side. His panned weapon hit three out of the four men almost immediately. The fourth danced backwards down the steps, but Big Jan rolled a grenade after him and hastened his end. Down below, the second four were attempting to push away from the mooring spot. The bursting grenade still took them by surprise, along with the falling bodies of their comrades.

The Dutchman wriggled forward to the top of the wall from which vantage point he lobbed another grenade. This time the 'pineapple' fell directly into the canoe which was obliterated by the second stunning explosion. Bodies floated, but none had the power to make a stroke.

Britwell fought down his reaction to the bloodshed. He crossed to the head of the stairs and studied the scene of carnage. He wanted to admonish Jan for destroying one of the canoes unnecessarily, but the sight of a turning decimated body put him off and he turned his attention to the swinging basket while his partner hauled out the intact canoe and gathered together all items of value.

He was weary again by the time they returned to the Aid Post. His thoughts had begun to get out of hand. He found himself wondering what the van Vliets were doing to him and the code by which he was supposed to live. Loving Christina meant sharing action with her blood-thirsty brother. He could not help thinking that those who live by the sword die by the sword.

★   ★   ★

The town of Oosterbeek reverberated constantly, as though it and the surround-ing hamlets were in the grip of a protracted earthquake. For the toilers in the Regimental Aid Posts, there was no let up. Work was work, and never ending. The Germans were regularly infiltrating the British perimeter. Every time they made progress, a great effort had to be made. Lives were lost due to the surprise moves: other casualties occurred during the frantic attempts to straighten out the lines and evict or eliminate the enemy.

The switching on of electric lights marked the passage of day for the medical teams. The radio communication with forces south of the river had appreciably improved. This meant that the allied artillery could be used to a greater extent to hold back the encroaching Germans on the flanks. A supply of D.U.K.W.s and other water craft had been asked for use between *Der Kessel* and the Poles, near Driel, but on that particular evening they had not arrived. The Poles were holding on to their south river territory adjacent to the polder, but no river crossings were attempted.

Night dragged on into day. Sunday morning. For those who worked in hospitals and Posts the tolling of the bells in churches a few kilometres distant marked the passage of a whole week since the allied sky troops appeared to try and safeguard the northern end of the corridor shortcut to the Ruhr and Berlin. The bells again.

In the basement of the Post where

Christina worked, the trio toiled over the laundry around ten o'clock in the morning. The bells had started Christina, in particular, thinking deeply.

Britwell, perceiving her mood, remarked: 'A penny for your thoughts, *Mejuffrouw*!'

Christina sniffed, stepping away from the hot soaking linen. 'I was thinking of Aunt Cora, that's all. I know we can't pick and choose, but I had hoped that she would survive all this — this bloodshed. Besides, she had a nice sense of family . . . '

Suddenly Jan whistled. 'Oh hell, sis, I'm sorry. I forgot to tell you. Aunt Cora's alive and well. Fitter than *we* are, if you ask me!'

'Then why the devil didn't you tell me, Jan?' the girl protested, pushing back her white hair band. 'Really, you have the most abominable manners. No sense of family! Where is she, then? And you'd better not be joking!'

Jan took hold of a white sheet and began to wring the foaming hot water out of it with his powerful hands. 'She's in her own house — what's left of it. In the basement. We were more or less standing over her the first time we looked, I suppose. Anyway, after Harry and I had collected that water on Friday I thought I'd have another look. And there she was! The air was bad down there. Not much daylight getting through, either. But she was just as fit as always, just as sharp-tongued, too. She gave me hell for not having visited her sooner when I was in the area.

'I had to go to work on the ventilation, all the time she was nagging me. Then I had to build a sort of shelter over the stair head out of some corrugated iron, so they could get out when they wanted, and the chores she wanted doing . . . phew! I never thought I'd finish, honestly!'

Britwell was prompted to say: 'Jan, you haven't made any mention of your folks. I'm sure you must have had time to ask about them.'

'Who were the other people down there with her, Jan?' Christina asked, as she wiped perspiration from her brow.

Big Jan hurled another sheet into a big wicker basket, stepped back and dabbed himself down with an old apron.

'You heard the railways went on strike last Sunday? Well, old Cornelis finished a spell of duty on Sunday morning. He went to Utrecht directly after church, collected your mother and went into hiding. Cora's not supposed to know where they are, but she reckons they may be with your grandmother in Apeldoorn. That's about all.'

Jan always referred to his father, Cornelis, who had married twice, as 'Old' Cornelis.

'And the others with Cora?' the girl prompted.

Jan shrugged. 'Oh, some little kid whose parents went to the coast. A girl about eight. Two old ladies, neighbours who were shelled out, and an elderly retired seafaring man — the one who's fancied her for years. He has a wooden leg, or is it a metal one?'

Christina nodded. 'What did Cora say about all this?'

Jan almost blushed. 'Oh, well I didn't really get the chance to talk to her about anything serious, sis. I mean I had to grab that bottle of apricot brandy before she changed her mind. I can still remember her walloping the dust out of my pants with a carpet beater, you know!'

Britwell thought: It figures. Christina gave her brother a long searching look and flared her nostrils at him. Jan stripped off his combat jacket and threw himself into the work with redoubled energy.

Both Britwell and the girl privately thought that Jan's most recent revelations couldn't fail to have an effect upon their immediate future.

★   ★   ★

That same afternoon a trip had to be made to the south bank for food and drugs. Jan heard about it by hovering near one of the local military H.Q.s. He held back on account of not having been popular on an earlier occasion, but when the weary British troops were reluctant to take on the chore, he volunteered and was accepted.

Britwell found himself signed on as

Jan's assistant. For the crossing, two flat broadly built rowing boats, left behind in a yard by Dutch people who had evacuated Noordelden, were brought into use. Two Border Regiment soldiers assisted them to get the boats to water. After that, Jan and Britwell were on their own.

No further attempts had been made to penetrate British territory from the river. Although the partners were wary of distant guns, their crossing to the south passed uneventfully, except for the vagaries of the boats. Jan's leaked in a couple of places, but the other was the more difficult to handle. It had a marked tendency to swing away to port. Crossing to the south side, the steering peculiarity helped in a small way to fight the current, but returning loaded with drugs, small arms ammunition and very basic food stores, the opposite was the case. In fact, the Polish medical officer, a tall dark theatrical major, sporting a King Charles I moustache and beard, panicked in the first few yards of the return trip as the Britwell boat swung acutely away to port in a downstream direction.

Britwell yelled out to Jan, who was ahead of him, and strained with all his strength to get the heavily-loaded craft back on course. His right arm ached with the effort and even then he was only just holding his own with the current and the boat's fault.

'Hold on, Harry!' Jan called back, when he saw the gravity of the situation. 'I'll throw the grappling hook!'

Britwell, meanwhile, capsized on his seat due to an excess of effort. He was on his knees when the rope with the iron-clawed hook whistled over and narrowly missed his head. Panting and breathless, he hooked it over the bow, well forward. Upwards of a minute passed, during which van Vliet's great strength held both boats against the current and enabled Britwell to get back to his seat and the oars which, fortunately, were still held by the rowlocks.

Blood vessels pounded in Britwell's temples due to the effort necessary for forward progress. At times, his sight was blurred. One thing acted as a relief. The Polish M.O. and his two orderlies had withdrawn from the bank, apparently convinced that the shipment would get through.

Under the north bank, Jan courageously turned up-stream, still towing the wayward second boat. Britwell recovered a little as his craft scraped the bank. He grabbed a metal ring, secured to it with the wet painter and flopped down on a couple of boxes to rest.

For the first time since the trio arrived he began to know real fatigue; the sort of tiredness which ordinary sleep, rest and food cannot immediately put right. Going up the steps, he swayed like a drunk.

'Why don't you call the red berets, Harry, then carry on to the Post? You look about all in!'

Jan's voice was harsh and hoarse, and yet it showed concern for his comrade. Still rather too far gone for any sort of conversation, Britwell nodded and moved off. Somehow his irregular feet found their way to the nearest paratroop H.Q. He relayed instructions as to how to find Jan and the boats, and then he was on his way towards the Post, moving like a tired animal, far from home.

He turned in on a door, resting on trestles. It was located in a spare room, and had been used as an emergency operating bench before the Germans took away many of the casualties by ambulance. For a time, in spite of his weariness, he did not sleep soundly. It was only when Christina found him an hour later, and kissed him, that the conditions were right for rest.

A little later still, the girl kicked off her shoes and snuggled close to him under the same blankets. She was wearily wondering if either or both of them would acquire a shroud in the near future.

18

Jan slapped the flat of his hand on the underside of the door bed around half past six the following morning. First Britwell and then Christina slowly sat up. Neither of them looked convinced that reality was reality and that they were all three still alive.

Jan had stripped off his combat jacket to wash. A soiled towel was draped round his neck. He nodded and grinned.

'Today is the day,' he whispered. 'I have talked to many soldiers, doctors and other people. Today is critical. I think this morning we three ought to take a little time off to talk to Aunt Cora. For me, she is too formidable in argument, but you, Christina, you could talk to her. She would have advice for us, tell us what to do at this critical time.'

Christina glanced frankly into Britwell's stubbled scowling face. He nodded. The girl also nodded, but to her brother who then moved away. The long legs, capable on merit of representing Holland in Olympic athletic events, slid to the ground. The girl stood up and stretched, arching her body like a ballet dancer and reminding Harry Britwell that he had still a lot to live for.

★　★　★

Jan clattered an old poker on the corrugated iron temporary entrance to Cora van Vliet Neeskens' residence.

'If that is you, Jan, come down here!'

Jan called: 'Yes, aunt.' He backed off a couple of paces, cautiously lowered the sack in which he kept his weapons and gave ground to his sister and Britwell.

Down below, the basement was lighted by candles and a paraffin lamp. Cora van Vliet's rocking chair was moving steadily as they negotiated the creaking stairs and adjusted their eyes to the lack of light. A small plump girl with pigtails was teasing out a simple hymn tune on a pipe recorder, punctuated rather heavily by an old man's wooden leg tapping on the top of the metal heating stove.

One old woman was sleeping in a worn armchair, wrapped in a shawl. The other's wrinkled fingers were busy with knitting needles. Cora snapped her fingers. The tortuous music and the tapping ceased. The child asked and received permission to go up the stairs and take a look around.

The old retired seaman withdrew his wooden limb from the dead stove, sharply examined the visitors through his short-sighted eyes and then withdrew into himself. Christina moved forward and embraced her aunt with great warmth. She was not put off by the old woman's rather gaunt features and somewhat chilling gaze.

Christina whispered to her, and Britwell was introduced. He retired to sit on an old family chest near one wall, while Jan moved forward and clumsily embraced his aunt. The girl sat at the feet of her aunt, and began to talk in quiet Dutch. Jan propped himself against a wall, folded his arms and waited to be admonished for something or other.

Every now and then, Cora asked questions. Britwell had an idea what was being said because of the gestures, the inclining of the head. At length, the conversation ceased and the rocking chair went into motion again. To Britwell, the old woman with the greying black hair and strong features looked to have abnormal powers: as if the future was revealed to her. Along with everyone else, he waited for advice from her.

Checking the rocker very briefly, Cora van Vliet spoke to her niece. Christina took off the white hair band which she had worn since the Aid Post. Her hair cascaded out around her shoulders and neck. She smiled and blushed shyly in Britwell's direction.

'My aunt says we are not to worry about her and these other folks with her. She advises Jan and me to go with you, get beyond the British lines south of the river. Run for safety is what she says. What do you think?'

It was a relief to hear the girl's voice in English again.

Britwell said: 'If I'd had my way you

would have run with me for safety long before this. I agree with her. Is it possible for me to speak a few words with her before we go?'

Christina chuckled. 'Of course. She understands English, but she is a little bit out of practice. Go ahead.'

Moving nearer, Britwell said: 'Mevrouw van Vliet, I wanted to say how sorry I am for the plight of the local people. How they have suffered since the paratroopers came! For years they have been hungry, and now at the very least their homes are pounded almost to rubble. They should not have suffered so.'

Suddenly Britwell dried up. Christina's shining eyes, however, made him think his short speech had been worth making. Cora van Vliet reached behind her for an old tin box which had once contained sweet biscuits. She retained it on her knee while she made her reply.

'Mr Britwell, my niece has told me how long you have been her friend, and how you came to Holland especially to look for her. That is good. Strong feelings make for a happy life. Those of us who are older, and live here, don't you worry about us. We are fighters. We have thrown off the yoke of other invaders before the Germans. And learned how to suffer. And we shall take up our battle with the sea again, as soon as this struggle is over. At the present moment, we are suffering from a surfeit of soldiers, Mr Britwell. But it will pass. Quite soon. So, if you have the chance, take my niece and nephew away with you for a time. Come back and visit in peacetime, or when the tide of war has gone beyond us. You will know when to come. I talk too much. Here, take a few of these.'

She opened the biscuit tin and showed him about a dozen expensive Dutch cigars, saved for better times. Britwell smiled and accepted the offer. He took six, and Jan was given two by hand a few moments later. The trio of visitors made the rounds of the cellar dwellers, and were very courteous as they left. Jan stayed behind long enough to do one or two essential chores for the old lady and then he was running to catch up with the other two.

* * *

Some three hours later, a doctor of their acquaintance ushered them into a local military H.Q. not far from Noordelden. Their work with stores, collecting water and chores at the hospital had made them known by repute over quite a big area of *Der Kessel*.

They were in time to hear a dissertation by a liaison officer from the Brigadier's H.Q. The officer concerned, wounded in the arm and bright-eyed with benzedrine to keep him awake, expounded the rules for withdrawal.

'Troops from various parts of the perimeter will start to pull out around 21.30 to 22.00 hours. Those furthest from the river will, where possible, start first. There will be a west route and an east route, each liberally marked by parachute tape. Guides will probably be glider pilots boosted by any locals who are still around and willing.'

The soldier listeners were in a sorry state. Every other one seemed to have suffered some sort of wound. Their hair was tousled. The air was full of their perspiration. Dark rings were making their eyes look hollow. Every man had a beard.

'We have some small stores, K-rations, brought over from the Poles yesterday. These will be distributed to the troops before they have to pull out, along with sulphanilamide and morphia. These latter, mostly for the men who are too far gone to move.

'The password, if anyone is challenged, will be John Bull. The actual crossing and the boats are the responsibility of the Royal Engineers. I feel sure they won't let you down. Any questions?'

★   ★   ★

2200 hours. The night was already dark. It was raining. The withdrawal had begun from the furthest groups of British survivors isolated to the north-west and north-east. Visibility was bad. A mere stumbling apart of five yards was sometimes sufficient for a man to lose touch with those ahead of him.

Here and there, the regular probing bullets of snipers found a target unexpectedly. As the small units converged, so the meadows up from the river bank became overcrowded by troubled and tired men: men whose nerves were almost at breaking point. Their muffled feet nevertheless churned up the earth and made it treacherous to tired feet.

Britwell, Christina and Jan started their part of the exercise from the ruined street of Noordelden where Cora van Vliet lived. Every now and then, they called instructions to one unit or another. The British, tired and lacking confidence, reacted well when they heard a friendly call, or saw the brief signalling flash of an electric torch. Presently, the same wounded officer from the main H.Q. came along. He stopped to talk to the trio.

'I hate to ask you to do more when we're withdrawing, but it seems some of our men haven't received the news about the withdrawal, and the password and such. Do you think you could make one more reccy up there and make sure everyone knows?'

Jan accepted promptly enough. 'Consider it done, major. We know the area as well as anyone, even though it's been pulverised lately.'

The officer gave a tired smile. He spoke to his sergeant who had been moving the shattered jeep downhill without use of the engine. A last supply of drugs and a few eatables were produced. Britwell took charge of them.

The major said: 'It'll be tough. There's no knowing when Jerry will realise we're on the move. If you get cut off, you could be done for. Down by the river, it'll be every man for himself. Good luck.'

Britwell and Jan shook his good hand and watched the silent jeep withdraw. Britwell's stomach began to rumble. He had a feeling that the critical time was at hand. If they all three separated and went off by different paths in that darkness and drizzle, what were the chances of all three coming out alive again?

He was slow to make a decision, and Christina did it for him. All three were togged out in their battle dress or forage clothes. The girl's tunic was worn inside out so that her orange circles did not attract attention.

'I'll take the north-east,' she remarked matter of factly. 'Jan, you go to the north-west. And for goodness' sake don't get the idea all over again that you're fighting a private little war. Harry, you go up the middle sector.'

Britwell nodded. He thought of asking one of them to draw him a sketch map of his territory, but he refrained from putting them to the trouble because there were so many flattened buildings, so many heaps of rubble and so many burnt out vehicles.

'How long will it take?' the Englishman asked, trying to keep the doubts out of his voice.

'About an hour, wouldn't you say, Jan?'

'Sure. About an hour.' Jan looked up from sorting out the hardware. 'Here's a Schmeisser for you, Harry, and a few magazines. Don't use it unless you have to. Also two grenades. I know you like British made explosives. And a bayonet. Take some of those drugs, and be on your way. Meet back here in about an hour. Okay?'

Britwell kissed Christina, shook hands with Jan and shouldered his gear. Christina was the first away, her long legs eating up the dusty ground in the plimsolls she kept for her training runs.

'So long, Big Brother,' Britwell murmured.

He sauntered off towards the north with a ringing Dutch oath from Jan echoing through his ears.

*   *   *

Words like dodgy, tricky, potentially lethal came to Britwell's mind as he went through his risky chore. Twice in the first half hour he was almost bayoneted by tired paratroopers who had forgotten the password and also the withdrawal plans and times. Others had not received the vital messages. Somehow, he managed to stay away from the business end of their weapons and get them organised. The drugs, he doled out as he thought fit, along with a few packets of cigarettes and the K-rations. The wounded who were not coming out were content just to chat with him.

One after another, he sent three small groups off down the middle withdrawal route. Just when he thought he had progressed as far north as the boundary a Spandau opened up perilously close. He threw himself down, and was guided by the return fire to yet another small pocket of British resistance which might very well have been overlooked.

He knelt down by a primitive bunker, said his bit about the withdrawal and the password, and was surprised to find that no one intended to evacuate. They had fought together for so long that the two who could have walked away refused to leave the others.

'Don't be embarrassed, laddie,' a Scottish voice advised. 'Just go back the way you came. Tell them you couldn't find us, or we don't like travellin' on the Sabbath, or something. And all the best to you an' yours!'

Britwell mumbled something appropriate. He wanted to do something special for the Scotsmen, but he was fifty yards away when he remembered Cora van Vliet's cigars and his nerves were such that he could not face going back with them.

The infernal noises were spasmodic, but none the less trying in the dark. Cannon shells, mortar bombs, tracer bullets pervaded the atmosphere like it was just another night of warfare. Not many of the red berets were left to return the fire. How long would it take for the Germans to know of the withdrawal?

Stumbling occasionally, Britwell hurried back to his rendezvous with the other two. In the last ten minutes of his hour, he was eagerly glancing to right and to left, knowing that his Dutch comrades ought to be on a converging course with him. A sudden whoosh followed by the ear-splitting crash of a mortar bomb burst distracted him. He stumbled over a manhole and rose on his knees as the explosion filled a street area east of Noordelden full of an eerie blue light.

He groaned. 'Goodness, Chrissy, keep clear of that sort of thing,' he murmured.

'Here's hoping those legs keep you clear of all trouble tonight.'

He was still down there, blinking and wondering when a diversion began south of the river. At almost the same time, artillery batteries on either side of the Polish territory began to open up and throw their missiles towards the north. Westerbouwing and Wolfheze suffered on the west side of *der Kessel* while other guns put down patterns of shells near small settlements like Den Brink and Mariendaal between Oosterbeek and Arnhem.

Britwell groaned again. He was sufficiently well versed in military strategy to know that this was a blind: a special shoot to make the Germans think heavy reinforcements were in the vicinity and preparing to cross the river from south to north. He wondered how long they would be hoodwinked: or if they already knew the truth.

★ ★ ★

2315 hours. The area east of Noordelden had been floodlit by the eerie blue light twice more when the shadow detached itself from the foot of a brick wall which had been reduced to three bricks in height.

'Christina, where the hell have you been, girl?'

The tone of Britwell's voice made it seem as if he was beside himself. In fact, for every one of the fifteen minutes since 2300 hours he had suffered. And here she was. Unscathed. Her magnificent hair was a shapeless bundle under an old beret. Her expression showed that she was tired, but that was all.

He hugged her to him and indulged in a long kiss, but after that she gently disengaged herself and stood quite still, listening intently: trying to separate out the different sounds of war.

'What about Jan?' she whispered.

Britwell shrugged. He knew that she would not move towards the boats until her brother appeared. He also knew just how unpredictable the big Dutchman was on occasions such as this. Three paratroopers and then another three appeared some fifty yards further west. They had been separated and were now acting almost like blind men in their weariness.

Britwell called: 'John Bull, hold on a minute.'

His intervention enabled the second trio to link up again with the first, but no one showed any sort of a reaction when he asked about the tall Dutch messenger. Christina came alongside of him. She mentioned her brother, one detail after another. In the dark, no one would have noticed his red hair, and this she appreciated: but a continuous shaking of the head over everything else made her spirits sink.

As soon as the escapers had gone from view, Britwell said: 'We'd better go and look for him. He's late.'

Christina was slow in answering. When she spoke, she insisted on going alone. Britwell was too tired to plead. He was also too tensed up to stay in the region of Noordelden alone. Before the girl was out of earshot, he called after her. 'I'm going to backtrack up the middle sector a little way, in case he's wandered and had an accident of some sort. You hear me, Chrissy?'

By way of an answer, she turned briefly upon her heel and waved to him. His heart felt heavy as he started north again. He wondered if that had been the big farewell — the last one.

★　★　★

Although he had this feeling perpetually now that time was running out for his two allies and himself, Britwell used as much caution as was possible as he moved back towards the north. Here and there, he stumbled and his mind groped back to where he had stumbled on the way down.

The horrible lingering stench of a burning German armoured car filled his nose, his tubes and his lungs till he coughed. He figured that the wind might have changed the direction of the smoke, but at least he had a vague notion of where he was. It was shortly after he had negotiated the smoke that he heard the unearthly deep-chested laugh. The timbre of it made him shudder. Surely, he thought, there was enough activity about in this God-forsaken area not to be thinking of ghosts and the like.

He paused, tilted back his head and listened. The fiendish laughter came again. He did not recognise the voice, but a sudden flash of intuition made him risk a brief cutting shout.

'Jan van Vliet! If you can hear me, indicate your position. This is H. B. Understand?'

A slight gurgling sound: a brief pause and then the return call.

'Over here, Harry. About two heaps of rubble to your left, I'd say. But mind how you come. I'm planning a few surprises for the sons of the Fatherland! You coming over?'

Britwell was pleased to know Jan had been located, but he felt no sort of pleasure as soon as he became aware that the big Dutchman was trying out a few specialities of his own. After just tripping over a yielding heap of rubble and almost prostrating himself in front of the crouching redhead, the Englishman was in no mood to humour his comrade.

'All right, Jan, don't bother to tell me what you're doing. I'll guess. You've begged, borrowed or stolen another bottle of strong liquor to keep your spirits up, and now you're laying booby traps. Trip wires, plastic explosive and all that, for when the Germans move down these paths. Great! I suppose you think you're something of a hero? A great guerilla fighter! Well, I don't.

'I'll give you that all the British in *my* sector have pulled out, but you must have put booby traps in your own sector first. Right? Over on the west side. Well, for your information, your little kid sister has gone dancing up there in her plimsolls, on her Olympic runner's legs. And what for? Because she refused to make for the river. Her beloved brother was overdue!'

While Britwell was filling his lungs to tongue-lash his partner, Jan van Vliet rose slowly to his feet. A huge groan escaped his lips, as the purport of what Britwell feared became clear to him. Nevertheless, he raised the apricot brandy bottle (one of his aunt's) to his lips and swigged from it heartily. In silhouette, he looked like a massively tall bugler sounding the alarm to arms.

'We must do something about Chrissy right away. I'm sorry I've thrown things late, Harry. Honest I am.'

'Damn and blast you, Jan, Chrissy could have her feet blown from under her before we have time to contact her! We may never see her again!'

Jan gave out like a wounded bull. He corked up his bottle, finished off what he had been doing at ground level, warned Britwell to keep away from the flickering streamers of marker tape, and moved a few steps further westward. After a few seconds of hesitation, he cupped his hands about his mouth and shouted.

'Chrissy, can you hear me?'

The cacophony of war was a continuing, wearing blasting *mélange* of sound, but somehow the great bull-roarer voice penetrated the orchestrated war noises and echoed to a small degree off some of the decimated houses. The two men stood stock still, as though fearing any sort of a reply. The seconds rolled by. Jan turned to Britwell and beckoned, but before they could move off, a sudden heart-jolting burst of Spandau fire came from a point perhaps a hundred yards north-west of them.

They winced and dropped, but it was not firing at them. Britwell's fears mounted. Jan murmured that there had been no sniper point in that direction when he was up there. He muttered something about the Bosches infiltrating from the west. Britwell gripped his arm.

'Don't come if you don't want to, but I have this awful feeling we have to investigate the cause of that last machine-gun burst. See what I'm getting at?'

Van Vliet's mouth was the second to dry out. Walking with infinite caution, they moved slowly towards the recent staccato noises. Scarcely detectable were the tiny sounds of the infiltrating Panzer grenadiers as they probed forward, more or less along the line of recent firing.

Yard by yard, the two forces came closer: but progress was slow. At last, Britwell saw something fluttering on the ground. He grabbed Jan firmly by the wrist and stopped him from falling over Christina's prone body. She had lost her beret. Her spilling hair, disturbed in the wind, had betrayed her presence. They knelt beside her. Britwell cradled her head. Jan opened up the liquor bottle.

'Chrissy, are you all right?' Britwell whispered.

She stirred, looked pained in the almost non-existent light, and then forced a smile. She pointed towards her left leg. Britwell was quick to react, but Jan pushed him aside and applied the bottle to her lips. The Englishman felt her leg. The ankle was at a strange angle. As he probed gently, a tiny spray of liquid crossed the back of his hand. She was *bleeding*!

Britwell said: 'Her ankle's shattered, Jan. And she needs a tourniquet! And we don't have any time in hand!'

'Let me have her, I'll carry her down to the boat! They'll patch her up on the other side!'

'No, I've got to fix the tourniquet first. She'll bleed to death otherwise.'

Jan gave in, and Britwell twisted a piece of cloth and applied the necessary pressure to the left thigh. Christina winced, but managed another brave smile.

The girl said sleepily: 'I've hurt my ankle, but it'll be all right now. Now you are both here!'

The unmistakable clatter of boots moving nearer. Jan grabbed his sister, adroitly placed her on his back and somehow achieved a fireman's lift. Jan moved away. He was able to walk almost soundlessly on an occasion like this when it was really necessary. The awful significance of that shattered ankle had not so far fully registered in Britwell's mind, but he was sufficiently angered over the injury to his sweetheart to hold back and do something about it.

A grenade. That would slow them. His hand was as steady as that of a veteran as he produced the explosive and toyed with it. Having pulled the pin, he almost spoiled everything by letting anger take over. In fact, he aimed the grenade quite a bit lower than was wise. Had it been another foot lower, it might have rebounded from a close wall and blasted off quite near.

As it was, the thrower was lucky. It fell

with an urgent plop among the infiltrators, caused a sudden scatter, and
accounted for four men. Britwell then ran
after Jan and his burden.

★ ★ ★

At midnight, the German commanders in
the area finally realised what sort of
movement was afoot. Accordingly, they
directed their artillery and automatic fire
into the area of the meadows just north of
the river. When it became clear that the
withdrawal was still going on shells
pitched into the river itself and also into
the wharves on the southern bank.

To counteract the lethal activity of the
enemy's guns, the British put up smoke.
This helped for a time, but the driving
rain and the wind hastened its dispersal.
More and more guns seemed to be
concentrating on the muddy meadows
which were the assembly area. Shells and
bombs and long curving bursts of bright
tracer made continued living a very
doubtful proposition for the badly battered, exhausted paratroopers who had

dropped from the skies as an elite corps scarcely more than a week earlier. The withdrawal could have been likened to a miniature Dunkirk.

One set of boats were manned by Royal Canadian Engineers. These took the form of strong wooden storm boats propelled by outboard motors. Against the current, however, they operated with pitiful slowness and presented easy targets to the gunners on the high ground around Westerbouwing, who merely had to aim their weapons along the comparatively narrow width of the river between two points.

There were no D.U.K.W.s available. The British field companies operating the other type of craft also had a tough job on hand. Their boats were of the collapsible assault type which needed to be paddled. At the outset, these craft had a crew of four. Later, when the current appeared to grow stronger, six men were needed, and later still they were manned by eight.

Paddled boats and powered boats alike suffered. The current swept them past the points of embarkation. Great gouts of water put up by exploding mortar bombs sent them ploughing into one another. Machine gun bullets scythed across the water and holed many of the frail craft.

As time went by, the scene became a macabre backcloth to violent death, a jungle of maniacal pyrotechnics which the devil could not have improved upon. Ashore, on the north bank, the access paths began to acquire a more permanent shape. In addition to the fluttering paratroops' marker tape, bodies populated the winding routes. Countless dozens of those who crouched in the muddied meadows did not live to rise up and take their turn in the boats.

Into this most turgid and hazardous of take-off points came Jan van Vliet with his sister on his back, followed closely by Harry Britwell. Jan stumbled from one sorry group of red berets to another. Every now and then an exploding shell showed where a boat was eliminated during the crossing. They were close enough to see that some men were so far gone as to rush the boats.

Britwell felt despair clutching at his

vitals. 'It's no use lining up with them, Jan! Chrissy needs queue priority. You'll have to think of something else. What about that canoe we took from the Krauts?'

Jan, whose back appeared to have permanently rounded under his burden, gradually straightened up as Britwell put the new suggestion to him.

'Think you can find the way to it, Harry?'

'We can try. If you like I can give you a spell at the carrying!'

Jan declined the offer. Britwell headed on in front, his eyes straining into the rainy gloom, his thoughts broodingly turned inwards. He wondered what they would do if someone else had discovered the hidden canoe before they got there. His nerves were on the rack. Ordinarily, the trip to the spot where the canoe had been hidden would only have taken a few minutes. In these circumstances, however, it took between fifteen and twenty minutes and the going underfoot never seemed easy.

Jan seemed to be talking to himself.

Britwell, at times, strained to hear. Eventually he heard enough to know what it was that bothered the troubled redhead. Christina was scarcely conscious, but he was talking to her.

'It wasn't me, Chrissy. Honestly. I didn't do it to you. It wasn't one of my booby traps. And what's more I wasn't drunk. But don't worry. We'll get you back across the Neder Rijin. And we'll find you a fine Dutch doctor, one who can fix your foot . . . make you as good as new. It'll be all right. Only you must believe me, it was a Spandau did the damage, not one of my little traps . . . '

After a time, shortage of breath made Jan dry up. Britwell staggered up a muddy slope between two low dykes and found himself on the cobbled area close to the scene of the encounter with the German raiding party. He waited for Jan to come up after him, and steadied the weary giant as he slithered near the top.

'I'll make for the steps. You get the canoe, Harry.' The voice was so hoarse it had changed its timbre. 'I hid it upside down in a narrow trench between two of the trees where the basket was caught. Go — go ahead.'

Britwell paused long enough to make sure that there was no activity about the steps. Having convinced himself, he began his search. Fate assisted him. His feet shot from under him when he was still seeking the trench and precipitated him into it. A certain amount of mud made the removal of the canoe a difficult task, but he managed it, straining to the utmost to do it without assistance from his partner.

It was too heavy to put it over his head and walk along with it, but he contrived to draw it clear and merely trail one end. Jan propped Christina on the stairs while the two of them manoeuvred the canoe down the steps and dropped it into the water. Into it went their weapons, and then the girl was hoisted into it. They laid her down along the bottom, between them. Jan took the bow and Britwell the stern. Both whispered a few words of prayer for their safety while they were still in the lea of the bank. And then they were off. Into the water gouts: into the endless streams of bright tracer bullets: between one procession of allied boats upstream and another downstream. The ripples on the surface buffeted them along after the explosions had churned up the water.

Jan's broad shoulders gave them great impetus. A near miss shot a boatload of soldiers upstream into the water. Jan ignored them, although they were scarcely thirty yards away. This time Britwell was not at variance with the Dutchman. Their craft was a frail one for this sort of work. They could not afford to take risks with Chrissy wounded between them. One or two clawing hands might have overturned the canoe and brought all their efforts to nought.

Britwell's ears assumed a permanent echo on the water trip as gouts of water flew up here and there and explosives banged incessantly. A few powerful waves threatened to sink them about a third of the way over. Jan cursed, until he managed to grab a floating helmet out of the river. With it, he baled manfully, while Britwell raised the pad under Chrissy's head with his insteps.

On again, but with greater hazard. By this time, tanks had penetrated the old British positions and machine gun crews had infiltrated almost as far as the embarkation point. Jan groaned, as a Spandau opened up from one of the new positions.

One of the collapsible boats, manned by six men and filled to capacity, was an early victim. The tracer bullets scythed into the seated men. Most of them ended up over the side. Bereft of its paddlers, the assault boat careered off course and bore down upon the flimsy canoe. Jan roared at it in English, but those who were still slumped in it were no longer of this world. He tried hard to avoid it. When it became clear that there would be a collision, he rose up cautiously in the bows and prepared to ward off the bigger boat.

At that moment, fate took a hand in the guise of one or two seemingly ill-directed bullets. One of them broke the paddle in Jan's hands, and the other just touched him on the outer side of his upper right arm. He retained his balance with a superb muscular effort and leaned towards the approaching bows.

His strength was sufficient to prevent a disastrous crash but the canoe tipped over to starboard. Jan fumed, saw a chance to improve their situation and growled a warning to Britwell. A few seconds later, he had managed to extract his body from one boat and achieved the other. As soon as the painter was attached, he worked like a maniac to toss the dead over the side in order to lighten the load.

Two thirds of the way across, with the canoe yawing off-course the lion-hearted Dutchman gathered himself for his greatest effort to date. In just a few strokes, he had righted the drift of the cumbersome assault boat and also taken the canoe in tow. Britwell worked steadily, although he was gripped by an unearthly nightmarish fantasy that it was all unreal.

One fine arc of tracer dipped towards Jan's boat from a set point. Another started to pan around, coming closer. Britwell had a premonition as to what was about to happen.

'Pull, Harry, and be ready to carry on alone!' Jan yelled hoarsely. 'And throw the sack over if you get a chance!'

As the deadly twin streams of tracer began to converge upon the assault boat, Britwell paused in his labours, dripping perspiration and rain. He hurled the sack which they had often made use of to keep their hardware in. Jan caught it, and sank back out of sight as the first of the tracers started to hit him.

Britwell groaned. A bullet parted the towing rope and threw him entirely upon his own resources. Meanwhile, Jan's fate hung in the balance. With three bullets having hit his trunk, the Dutchman still managed to hurl one grenade from an unheard of position. One Spandau ceased firing abruptly. And then Jan was on his feet again, his boat no longer controlled. It had been riddled below the waterline, around the stern. Clasped like toys, one in each hand and gripped under his arms, were the two Schmeisser machine pistols.

Under the impact of still more tracers he rocked like a drunkard, his bullets arcing away first to one side and then to the other. His knees were giving out and his magazines running low when, with a last determined despairing effort, he managed to home his guns on the other machine-gun.

The second hostile weapon cut out just as sharply as the first. At the same time, Jan sank to the boards, coinciding with the gradual sinking aft of his boat. The big Dutchman managed to claw himself up on the gunwale for a few seconds. He forced his boyish infectious grin, called: 'Take her across, Harry!' and ungrudgingly gave up his ebbing life.

With a big effort, Britwell avoided the sinking craft. He knew that his remaining energies would not last long. He put all he had into heaving the canoe towards the friendly shore. *Jan was dead . . . Was Christina still alive? The van Vliets came in pairs. Was he to lose them both on the same evening?*

Something brushed past his face. He ignored it, so intent was he upon making the best use of his failing energies. It was a rope, thrown by a watchful Pole. A loudly shouted instruction in Polish had no effect upon him. Finally, a Polish voice speaking fractured English communicated with him.

'For Chrissakes, man, grab the rope and be hauled in!'

Britwell complied. The bows swung out of line, but those who were hauling did a good job and in a few seconds the canoe was alongside. Willing hands were directed by him to remove his precious burden. Somehow or another he lost track of the following half hour.

He came to in a big house, and found himself in a large room holding several of the padded trolleys used to ferry surgery patients into operating theatres. Christina was stretched out on the trolley nearest to the doors with the round portholes in them — the ones which gave access to the theatre.

Suddenly, he was fully conscious: back in the land of the living and actually bathing the forehead and neck of his sweetheart, who was pale and drawn looking but nevertheless recovered sufficiently to open her eyes and know what was going on.

The swing doors opened. Two men in white overalls came through. One pointed to Christina and withdrew, the other remained in the background, watching. After a time, Britwell became aware of him. The slightly theatrical cast of features terminated by a tight white skull cap seemed vaguely familiar. He remembered the Polish M.O.'s facial hair.

Two firm-looking but compassionate nurses moved in upon Britwell, taking away from him the bowl of water and the sponge. Then the surgeon came over to him and took him by the arm, ushering him firmly but gently towards a waiting room.

'Come along, soldier. You rest out here. This is one hell of a time and place to carry on a courtship, don't you think? All right, you don't need to answer. I've examined your girl. It'll mean removing the foot, amputating. Serious, isn't it? But you have the look of a man whose love can take a setback like that. I think I can promise you she'll survive. Eh?'

Britwell nodded, smiled jerkily and started to weep. The surgeon called for someone to see to his needs. The war correspondent wanted to tell the kindly fellow why he was weeping, but just at that time he didn't seem to have the stamina necessary.

After all, it would have taken a long time to explain how a girl athlete had dreamed of nothing else for nearly eight years, nothing else except representing her country, Holland, in the running events of a peacetime Olympic Games.

THE END

We do hope that you have enjoyed reading this large print book.

Did you know that all of our titles are available for purchase?

We publish a wide range of high quality large print books including:
Romances, Mysteries, Classics
General Fiction
Non Fiction and Westerns

Special interest titles available in large print are:
The Little Oxford Dictionary
Music Book, Song Book
Hymn Book, Service Book

Also available from us courtesy of Oxford University Press:
Young Readers' Dictionary
(large print edition)
Young Readers' Thesaurus
(large print edition)

For further information or a free brochure, please contact us at:
Ulverscroft Large Print Books Ltd.,
The Green, Bradgate Road, Anstey,
Leicester, LE7 7FU, England.
Tel: (00 44) **0116 236 4325**
Fax: (00 44) **0116 234 0205**

MR. WALKER WANTS TO KNOW

Ernest Dudley

Mr. Walker, the Cockney rag and bone man, is always bumping into other people's troubles. After the murder of old Cartwright in the jeweller's shop, he becomes involved in adventures with his friend Inspector Wedge of Scotland Yard, with the arrest of a crooked police officer, and the escape of Cartwright's killer. Then there is another death — in Mr. Walker's own sitting room — but his problems are just beginning, as he discovers that he himself is a candidate for murder!

SCORPION: SECOND GENERATION

Michael R. Linaker

The colony of deadly scorpions at Long Point Nuclear Plant was eradicated. Or so people thought . . . Over a year later, entomologist Miles Ranleigh receives a worrying telephone call. A man has been fatally poisoned by toxic venom, identical to the Long Point scorpions' — but far more powerful. Miles and his companion Jill Ansty must race to destroy the fresh infestation. But this is a new strain of scorpion. Mutated and irradiated, they're larger, more savage — and infected with a deadly virus fatal to humans. And they're breeding . . .

THE RITTER DOUBLE CROSS

Frederick Nolan

In Nazi Germany, in 1941, there was a factory in the north German town of Seelze. Though officially its function was a top military secret, it was known to be associated with the manufacture of poison gases. Until a raid put the factory out of action . . . Based on fact, this is the story of five men who were parachuted in to Seelze to destroy the chemical plant. But the Gestapo were waiting — and one of the five was a traitor . . .

THE TRAVELS OF SHERLOCK HOLMES

John Hall

Secrecy surrounds the supposed death of Sherlock Holmes in 1891 — and his re-emergence three years later. What happened to him during the missing years of his life? This story of those missing years reveals how Holmes foiled his old adversary and became involved in a terrible game; its prize, the mastery of an entire continent — India. Holmes' adventures take him to Tibet, Persia and the Sudan, but as sole representative of the British Government, his life and the British Empire is at stake.